KYLE MUNTZ'S

Scary People

ERASERHEAD PRESS
PO Box 10065
Portland, OR 97296

www.eraserheadpress.com

ISBN: 978-1-62105-206-7

Printed in the USA.

Scary People

KYLE MUNTZ

ERASERHEAD PRESS
Portland, Oregon

List of Episodes:

—The first 30 pages

—Siguard bakes a cake

—The holy war

—Where the darkness is

—Stuff that happens when it is snowing outside
(an interlude)

—Onto the dust, the waves: a bridge between spaces,
which aren't...

—Teeth, corpses, dandelions, pt 1

—Final dungeon adventure fantasy quest

—Teeth, corpses, dandelions, pt 2

—The part with the aliens and the children

—Evisceration; the silence

The first 30 pages

30 is a good number.

I really hate cupcakes.

The first time I met Mathew, it was because both of us had walked into the same classroom. It was an awful experience, so by the time it was over we had a weird bond, like soldiers.

Mortar flew through the sky and many, many days were wasted. Our comrades were slain, one by one, until they became lumps of dust upon the ground.

Mathew is my best friend. He has a problem. But I'll get to that eventually.

Both of us were students at The School. It was the only school in The City.

I've been a student for a very long time.

Sometimes I meet some really weird people.

The first time I saw the alien, he was in a park. It was strange, because he was sitting on a bench, staring at children. Green fluid leaked out of something that might have been his mouth. I'm not sure what was going on.

In front of him, a group of children were playing. They tossed a ball in the air and laughed or whatever.

Every time they moved, his head(s) would follow them.

He drooled.

"Hello," I said.

The alien shook a little. He was wearing a suit, and he looked partly human, except tentacles came out from where his hands should be, and his eyes were yellow glowing bulbs, amidst *something*.

"So…" I said, "is it just me, or are you staring at children."

"Yes," he said. "They make me hungry."

"Like, your stomach?"

He shook his head—and one of his tentacles stiffened.

It turns out, all aliens are pedophiles. They came to The City to steal our children.

There must be something wrong with this universe.

"You kind of stand out," I said. "In a crowd, I mean."

"Do I?"

He shifted uncomfortably, and put his wrists together though the tentacles still showed.

"I just like looking at children," he said.

For a while after that, I walked through the crowd, asking everyone if I could borrow a rocket launcher.

No one had theirs on them, unfortunately.

I've always despised sitting in classrooms.

One day, when I was sitting in class, somebody came in late. He had his hair tied back like a samurai, and he was wearing a white t-shirt.

Usually it wouldn't have been so strange, except he had a sword too, in a sheath strapped to his side.

He stood there for a while, and I still couldn't get used to his t-shirt.

The teacher paused. He had that look I recognize, from being late so many times. Except usually I'm sly about it, so I get noticed less.

I am not a samurai.

When the samurai didn't move (it was really awkward, to be honest), the teacher said, "And you are?"

The samurai brought his hands together and bowed.

"My name is Hideyoshi Nakamura," he said. "I am a warrior."

…Silence.

The teacher coughed.

"Would you like to take a seat?"

Everyone shifted uncomfortably in their chairs. The

teacher obviously hadn't seen many samurai movies.

When another cough didn't work, he cleared his throat. Something was caught in it, but not really. In one hand, he brandished his eraser like a sword.

"Are you sure you're in the right place?" the teacher said. "I'm trying to give a lecture here."

I sighed.

A moment later, the teacher had no head.

Later we found out the samurai had been in the wrong classroom after all.

In the wake of the teacher's death, I now had a beautiful, beautiful conversation piece. No one had liked him very much, so there were lots of celebrations now that he was dead.

For a few days, I became extremely popular. Then, I got tired of the story, so I wrote it down. Multiple other versions existed, but mine became the definitive one.

Eventually, reenactments were filmed. In each of them, I made an appearance. Because of their popularity I ended up making some money, even if it wasn't very much.

This is how I became a writer.

I was being bullied by a girl. I've spent my entire life being beaten up by girls. I am frightened of them, because they're so much more dangerous than me.

I'm exaggerating, but Karen was sort of like that. A little.

When we went to the premier of my movie, she told me that for today we were dating. We weren't, because if we dated she would kill me in like two minutes, but I didn't have any power, because she was herself.

She held onto my arm and pressed her boobs against my shoulder. Every few minutes she bit me on the neck. The back of my shirt was all stained with blood, but I guess nobody noticed.

No one recognized me, of course. Because I was just the writer, I was only a name in the credits—so not only did no one care, they had no appreciation of my prose.

This was not a real theater. This was a building usually used for classes with a projector on one wall and a bunch of chairs lined up on the floor.

Karen and I sat near the back. I knew we'd reached a place she liked when she took her foot and stepped on mine really hard. It hurt all night, and later I found out she'd broken three of my toes.

Karen is too dangerous. Karen is too beautiful. If she looked like the person she was inside, I'm not sure what would happen.

"Look at everyone," she said. "They're all here for you!"

"Something like that."

"You don't sound very excited."

"The last time I went to one of these," I said, "it was a very loose adaptation. Instead of taking place in a classroom, it had been relocated to the Siberian wilderness. There were saber-toothed tigers involved. There was something very, very wrong with it."

"Charming."

She put her head on my shoulder and her hair was soft.

"Are you happy to be here with me?"

"I suppose."

She set her hand on my thigh. It felt nice, but I was afraid to say anything. Sometimes she would hit me just for breathing.

"You look cute today," she said.

"Oh. Thanks."

"If I could," she explained, "it would make me happy to take off all your clothes, tie you up, and leave you in a room for days, then come back later, while you were starving and thirsty, and feed you vinegar on the end of a sponge." She squeezed my thigh. "After that, we could experiment with things. It would be fun, I swear."

"No," I said. "No, I'll pass."

She moved back, and I thought about her lips.

She said, "That hurts my feelings, you know."

"It's not you. It's me. I really don't like the taste of vinegar."

"You're missing out."

"Yeah," I said. "I guess I am."

In the end, this adaptation was another failure.

It took place in space, on some sort of intergalactic battlefield. All the characters had been replaced by pastel colored things that looked sort of like squid, but with creepy human faces. I'm not sure how it related to what I'd written at all.

Mathew is a strange person. Sometimes his parents visit but he always finds excuses not to let them into his room, which is probably a good idea.

He doesn't like people knowing, but Mathew is utterly in love with pornography. He spends hours a day looking at penises; the rest of it he spends looking at vaginas. Every surface of his room is littered with pictures of naked people and pictures of dead goats.

That's why I never go into his room. I really hate goats.

Other than that, I guess he's pretty normal.

Mathew has a beautiful friend named Michelle. Michelle is much nicer than Karen. She has blonde hair and when she talks to me she doesn't make me feel bad about myself.

Karen is Mathew's sister. There must be something wrong with their family.

I've always thought Michelle was nice, but she's also really shy. Usually she's the one in the corner of the room, who keeps her head down and doesn't say much. But we're really good friends anyway, even if there's always something mysterious about her; something that isn't being said.

Sometimes Michelle sits and watches pornography with Mathew. They'll watch pornography all afternoon and then eat Chinese food.

There are worse ways to spend time, I suppose.

Michelle and I decided to start a garden. The idea was to be in touch with nature, or something.

We went outside someplace and found the ground. After that, we stuck seeds in it. We poured water on the seeds to see what would happen.

A stalk appeared, bending under its own weight. On the stalk was a sheep.

It took a few minutes, but eventually, the sheep climbed down, and started eating grass.

I wish life were a series of vignettes, instead of a sequence of memories.

It would make things so much easier, sometimes.

There was a killing spree going on. Originally I thought it must be the samurai, but when someone's cut to death with a sword, you can sort of tell.

Instead, people were turning up mauled and unrecognizable. I won't describe the corpses because they aren't something you want to look at, so they probably wouldn't be good to read about either.

The serial killer liked to kill children and eat their livers. He was even worse than the aliens, since at least the aliens don't eat people's livers.

All the prostitutes are dead, so now there's no one left to eat but children.

"You know," Mathew said. "I'm not sure I feel safe anymore."

"Hmm," I said, while playing video games. "I'm not worried."

"Why? People are dying—like, on the streets where we walk home and stuff. A kid got eaten in Michelle's back yard."

"I'm the main character," I said. "There's no way I would get taken out so early."

What I didn't say:

Mathew, on the other hand, might have something to worry about.

In class, they warned us to be careful walking home. Mostly the victims were still children, but the killer had also taken to people wearing fedoras. And he had a thing for eating dogs.

Even the last prostitute had been killed. He'd been walking a dog, and wearing a fedora.

His name used to be Jerry.

The general consensus, I guess, is that serial killers exist because young people play too many video games.

I opened my door one day and saw Mathew standing outside it, except he didn't have a face anymore. In its place was only a fountain, and blood.

"Nooooooo!!!!!" I exclaimed. "Did the serial killer get you too?"

"Sorry," said a voice from above. "That's my fault."

He'd accidentally let an anvil fall out of his window.

All of us gathered in one place for Mathew's funeral. As students at The School, none of us had any money—the closest we came was old candy wrappers—so we had to do it ourselves, on a hill within walking distance of the apartment complex, near the edge of a forest.

It was a green place, because there was grass growing on it, and the sun cried melancholic tears.

Mathew was in the ground, and all of us were standing above him.

Michelle was crying. Karen was sending a text message.

"What should we do?" I asked. "I've never been good at this."

Michelle sobbed slower, for a second.

"You should give a speech," she said. "You knew him best."

"I don't think I can," I said. "People always tell me I'm a terrible orator."

I looked at Karen for support, except instead all she did was hit me in the face.

Hard. I think my nose might have broken.

"All right," I exclaimed. "Shit."

"That's very considerate of you."

Ok.

"Before I start," I opened, "does anyone have any comments they would like to make?"

"The last time I talked to him," Michelle said, "he told me that in the event of his death, all his possessions would go to you."

"Err," I trailed off. "That's all right. You can have them."

"No, he insisted, really."

"So do I."

What we could have done, I realized, is have one of those old style funerals like they have in movies, where they burn the body on a pier, except we could have made the fire from pictures of naked people. I think he would have liked that: for his ashes to be engulfed by throbbing cocks and flaming vaginas.

"Karen," I asked. "Do you have anything?"

"Yes." She nodded. "I'm glad our parents aren't here right now, because they would be very disappointed in him."

"...Is that all?"

"One more," she said. "Even though he was always watching porn, I never caught him masturbating. I am very thankful for this."

"All right. That's enough, don't say anything else."

"My brother and I have an entire life behind us! I've known him longer than anyone else."

"No," I said, "just be quiet, you're ruining this."

She tried to hit me again, but I dodged.

I looked at the ground, where history was.

"I'm not sure how long we've been here," I said, "but for all that time, Mathew has been my best friend. He made life a little more bearable. There's nothing more important a friend can do."

After that, there was really nothing to say.

All of us were silent, and we spent quite a while just staring at the ground.

I spent the next few weeks watching pornography with Michelle. Unfortunately, she said it just wasn't the same.

When I said 30 pages, I was kind of just estimating.

Siguard bakes a cake

I didn't really expect this to happen, but I found out the serial killer was someone in my anatomy class named Siguard.

It happened by accident, which isn't a surprise. Everything in this life happens accidentally.

He had long hair. He was Scandinavian as fuck.

I'd never made the connection before, but I should have known it was strange for someone to be drooling the whole time in an anatomy class.

Siguard's face is like the pimpled crest of a Nordic rock, salt-stained by many waves.

He had never played a video game in his life.

Siguard liked to watch children's shows and musicals. He had a tendency, from time to time, to break out in song, no matter where he was at.

His voice was hideous.

One time, basically for no reason, Siguard handed me a piece of paper. His desk was right next to mine, so no matter how hard I tried to ignore him, it didn't work.

He sort of giggled. He winked at me.

"*It's a song I wrote*," he whispered. "*Tell me what you think.*"

Please no.

There are few things I hate more than reading things written by human beings, but Siguard especially.

"*I'll do it later*," I said.

He clasped his hands and said, "*Puhleeeease?*"

I gave in because I never, ever wanted to hear him make that sound again.

There were words on the piece of paper. This is what they said.

Siguard Bakes a Cake

My name is Siguard.
Tonight I will go home and bake a cake
out of children's fingers.

I like cake because it
is fluffy, especially when there are knuckles in it.

I am happy
because I am eating a cake
made out of children's fingers.

He grinned.

"What's this?" I asked. "It's not even musical."

"Every word," he said, wiggling his finger, "is true."

"Oh," I said.

"So," I said, later that day, "I think I might have some idea who's been killing people and eating their livers."

"That's nice," said Michelle.

"Yeah." I nodded. "That's what I thought."

She was doing homework, so I doubt she was really listening to me.

No one listens to me much, I've noticed.

"Do you know," she asked, "what percentage of taxes are allocated towards the preservation of City monuments?"

"No," I said, "not off the top of my head."

We were sitting in my room. The day felt like it was over already. I was thinking about other things I needed to do, and trying to figure out how I would deal with the consequences of not doing them.

Somehow.

"I wonder," she said, "what percentage of the population are really aliens."

"Too many," I said. "It's the tentacles that give them away."

"What are you planning to do tonight?" I asked.

She shrugged.

"If you want," I continued, "we could go hunting serial killers. The only problem is it might be a little dangerous. But whatever."

"Sure," she said. "I don't have anything better to do."

In order to look the part, we put on cool clothes and grabbed a pair of baseball bats.

Neither of us liked baseball, but we just had them, I guess.

"We should get Karen," Michelle said. "She's the most dangerous person we know. She could help."

"Maybe not," I said. "If we took Karen with us, she would probably kill somebody."

"Right, that's a good point. Maybe we should avoid her on the way out."

"Yeah, you're right, we should."

On the way out, we ran into Karen, and it was ironic. I have no idea what she was doing here.

"Oh," she said. "Hi."

"Hey," I said.

Michelle waved.

"What are you guys doing?" Karen asked.

"Sex," I replied. "And violence. You know."

"Yeah," Michelle said.

"That's nice," Karen said. "Would it be all right if I came?"

"Umm," I said.

"Sorry," Michelle said. "It's just us."

"Yeah. Collateral damage and stuff. Because of that time you broke my jaw when we were golfing."

"Oh." Karen said. "That's sad." She turned to me. "And you're pathetic."

"Right. I've come to terms with it."

"Don't be anxious." Michelle patted me on the head. "I'm used to it."

"That's very considerate of you."

I'm glad we made it away alive.

I don't think it will surprise anyone to know we didn't find anything. Instead, we spent the night eating ice cream and seeing a movie. Then we went to the park, like little kids, except we were bigger than that, a little, so we didn't know what we were doing there.

The next day in class I asked Siguard, "You're the one, right? Who's always eating people's livers?"

"Oh." He twiddled his thumbs and his face split, from ear to ear, literally, in a grin. "You've got meee!"

"Umm, like, why are you killing people?"

"Because they taste good," he said, with another smile.

"Don't you know that killing is pretty much morally reprehensible and stuff?"

"Hmm." He paused. "I'd never really thought of that."

He wouldn't have, I suppose.

That day, after class, I was walking through The School when I noticed it was full of corpses. Arms and hands and other body parts and stuff were laying all over everywhere.

I was thinking mainly that somebody needed to call a doctor.

In one of the rooms I saw the samurai, cutting people in half. I found out later he'd been challenged to a duel by the whole lacrosse team, and things just kind of went from there.

I was almost outside the building when I ran into Karen. I don't know what she was doing there, because she wasn't even a student, but whatever.

From behind me came the sounds of screams and scraping metal. Spraying guts and slurping bodies, that kind of stuff.

In general, everything pretty much sucked.

"Hey," I said. "Unless you really want to, I'd suggest staying outside. Bad things are happening in there. Like, death."

Her face sort of lit up—and I don't mean with light, I mean with fire.

"Really?" she said. "Don't worry, I'll take care of it."

"Seriously," I said. "It's dangerous."

"I'll be all right." She was already moving forward. "Just give me a few minutes."

I don't know. It was kind of cool how excited she was.

Fifteen minutes later, everything was quiet. I knew I shouldn't have, but I decided to go inside again.

Everything was carnage. The floor was soaked up to my knees in blood, so I had to wade through it to walk anywhere, and the samurai had killed all of the tennis players in The School as well.

This would require many, many Band-Aids.

Karen had the samurai tied to a desk in one of the classrooms, and she kept whipping him while stomping on his testicles. His skin was all covered in red welts. The screams were muted because of the gag she'd put in his mouth.

He writhed in pain (though he seemed to be enjoying it), and shook each time her foot touched his nuts.

Originally I thought everyone in the room with them was dead, but there was someone else in the far corner.

It was Siguard, and he had his face buried in one of the corpses.

Karen said: "That's what you GET, you WORM, you fucking WORM, don't even LOOK at me, you should just DIE, you fucking SCUM."

When I tried saying something to her she didn't hear

me. I was afraid to get any closer.

Finally, she yelled, "What?"

"You see that guy over there?" I pointed to Siguard. "The one eating that girl's liver?"

"Yeah," she said. "What about him?"

"He's the one who's been eating people's livers. Probably it's worth getting him too."

She paused to punch the samurai in the face one more time.

"Oh," she said. "Right, thanks."

I stepped back, because I didn't want to get in her way.

I don't think Siguard could have prepared for what happened next. One second he was doing his thing, then the next Karen was elbowing him in the mouth, and fighting a boxing match with his balls. She headbutted him in the nose and shattered it. She suplexed him into a nearby table. Then she picked him up and broke him in half against her knee.

She dragged him to the front of the room and tied him up next to the samurai.

When I got back to my apartment, Mathew was on my couch, eating potato chips. It made me kind of angry, because that was basically all the food I had. But I'd had enough violence today, so I decided just to let it go.

"What's up?" he asked. "I heard something strange was going on at The School."

"Your sister," I said.

"Tell me about it." He ate another potato chip. "You're not the one who had to grow up with her."

"No, I mean, really."

"When I would make her angry," he said, "she would beat me up, pull out all my hair, and toss me into the river naked, so that no one found me for about a week. She once broke both of my hands because I stole her grape juice."

"Oh," I said. "I suppose I shouldn't be surprised."

"Yeah." He ate another potato chip. "The rule is that you can usually depend on her to be worse than you expect."

"Was she always like that?"

"You'd have to ask her." He shrugged. "This is the way I always remember her."

"I feel sort of sorry for you, man."

"It's all right." He lifted the bag above his head, in order to get the last little pieces. "I'm used to it.

I decided I'd forgive him, just this time.

"So," he said, "I heard that while I was gone, you were spending quite a bit of time with Michelle."

"Yeah," I said. "I did."

"I suppose that's the way it goes. Before you got back, I finished putting most of my stuff back into my room. That's why I was here in the first place."

"Sorry for your traumatic experience, man."

He nodded. "Yeah, from now on I'm going to be very careful of falling anvils."

"We all make mistakes."

"Maybe," he said. "Some of us more than others."

Eventually Michelle came over as well. Mathew and I were temporarily not friends, because we were playing video games. She sat behind us and watched.

He won, and then I won, and then he won, and then both of us decided we really hated this game.

"Why do you guys even do this?" Michelle asked. "As soon as you start all you ever do is argue."

"It's part of being a man," Mathew said. "Playing video games is a manly thing."

Mathew used the word "manly" a lot, and then he would start complaining about football.

The only thing worse than football is the kind of racing where all they do is drive around in a circle.

It just bugs me.

"Oh yeah," I said. "Michelle, did you hear about what happened today."

"No, what?"

"Karen caught the killer and kicked him in the face. She also got the samurai, the one I wrote the story about, because he was killing people too."

"Yay," Michelle said.

"It was really badass," I said, "but I'm kind of afraid. I've never seen her like that before."

"Don't worry about it," said Mathew from across the room. "She likes you. You'll be all right. Probably."

"I keep turning her down though. You don't think anything will happen, will it?"

He put his hand against his chin and made a smart thinking face. "You'll survive. Most likely."

"That's very encouraging."

"Just be careful. She can smell your fear."

The door opened, and Karen came inside. She smiled. All her clothes were covered in blood

"Hey guys." She carried a plastic bag in one hand— she'd stopped at a supermarket to get sushi afterwards. It was the only food any of us had bought in like weeks. "What were you talking about?"

I'm not sure why, but for some reason, I picked up a pillow and began throwing it at the wall, over and over, so that it fell down but didn't bounce anywhere.

It was just a pillow. The sound it made wasn't even very loud.

"I figured we should celebrate," she said. "I've been awarded a medal of honor for contributions to The School."

"Congratulations," Mathew said.

"That's awesome," I added.

"You're the best," said Michelle.

"Also," said Karen, "I brought someone with me. I thought you would all like to meet him."

I hadn't noticed, because I'm dumb, but there was someone standing outside the door.

It was the samurai. He was covered in blood too, but mostly bruises.

"初めまして" he said, and bowed, and told us his name, which I forgot again immediately.

"Nice to meet you too," I said.

"Yeah, definitely," said Mathew.

"I like your hair," commented Michelle.

"Everyone," said Karen, "the polite thing to do is bow."
We bowed.

"Hideyoshi is a very interesting person," Karen told us. "I'm sure we'll all enjoy learning about him."

"Of course," we said.

Really though, the samurai never did talk much. I'm not sure if it's because he didn't like us, or maybe it was just his personality.

For reasons that will later be explained, except Karen, none of us ever called him by his name. Anywhere else, he would be referred to as a *deus ex machina*, but mostly I'll explain that later too.

"All right," I said. "Well, today will be interesting."

"You know," said Mathew, creeping towards the far side of the room, "I sort of feel like playing video games again."

"Yeah." I nodded. "Me too."

It's sort of disturbing how frequently I'll look out my window and notice children (with their parents or in groups or alone, whatever) being followed by aliens.

Usually the aliens are just standing a few feet behind them, creeping down the sidewalk with big, throbbing tentacles sticking out from their trench coats; but the children never notice, and it's weird.

Again, I never have a rocket launcher when I need one.

The next day, in class, Siguard was still there, except he looked really beat up. All his teeth were broken, and he couldn't walk straight anymore. When he grinned, his mouth looked like a window with all the glass shattered in it.

I'm still trying to figure out if this is a happy ending.

The holy war

This part of the story is going to be boring, because Mathew and I are the only main characters in it. It happened a long time ago, before we spent all of our time with Karen and Michelle.

A story without girls in it is a waste of time. Probably I could stop right here, since no one will be interested, but I suppose I should keep going.

I was getting tired of walking down the street. Not necessarily because of the road, but because there were always so many mobs on it.

Not mobs like you usually think of them, but middle-aged men in cheap suits with their hair parted down the middle, and middle-aged women wearing tacky dresses and ridiculous makeup and lots of jewelry.

Some had even brought their children.

All of them were carrying clubs, or hammers or pickaxes or whatever. The children generally had sharpened sticks, but I saw one of them carrying a lampshade, and another hitting people with his lunchbox.

They were hunting prostitutes. All of them were hunting prostitutes.

I'm not exactly sure how it happened, but someone, somewhere had decided that it was time for war, because prostitutes are evil.

This was the beginning of The Prostitute Genocide, which assured that lots of prostitutes would never have sex, ever again.

Another problem: for the most part, the mobs had a very poor sense of aesthetics. Both sides of the streets, almost everywhere, were lined with crucified prostitutes.

The majority of the victims were not happy about this. Usually they would call out for help, but it was really dangerous, because if you got caught helping them you would be stoned to death. That's why there were always people in every mob carrying big rocks, and quite a few smaller ones as well.

In general, I did my best not to go outside.

There was a big group of people ahead of me, standing around someone and hitting him with sticks. It was sort of like a dramatic scene in a movie, except without the cameras and music, and the drama.

The weird thing: the victim was someone I recognized. I wasn't sure where from at first, until I realized I'd sat next to him in class for a while.

His name was Mathew, and eventually he would become another main character of this book.

What happened, I guess, is that when he went in to buy a blowup doll with a famous person's face (apparently he needed a new one every few weeks, except it was a problem because he always tried to pay with pictures of dead goats), the owner of the store already had a screwdriver sticking out of his neck. Then someone threw a grenade into the store, and Mathew had to dive through a window all movie-like, except that hurt way more in real life, and pieces of glass got stuck in him.

He was surrounded. Mathew stood up, picking shards of glass out of his forearms, so that tears of blood leaked down over his elbows.

"Mommy?" said one of the children. "Is he evil too?"

The mother patted her son on the head. "Yes son," she said. "Everyone who enters this place becomes a very evil thing."

"Yay!" The son held his hand into the air, and I noticed he was holding a squirt gun—except, instead of water, it was full of acid.

The insides of the plastic sizzled.

The crowd was closing in around Mathew. One of them was holding a condom that had been lit on fire, waving it around on a stick like a flag.

"Oh no!" I shouted, pointing towards the other end of the street. "Look at that mechanical prostitute!"

I can't believe that worked, but yes, the entire crowd ran to attack the other way. While the children squirted Mathew with acid, I'd snuck into the store, taken the last blowup doll, put a bucket on its head, and posed it on the roof of a car with its legs out to either side.

I went to help Mathew up. Little patches of his skin sizzled, and he was bleeding from a wound above one of one his eyes. A child had tried to scrape them out through his skull, except all that happened was he started to bleed.

"Thanks a lot," he said. "I know you, don't I? We're in class together."

"Yeah," I said. "That's me."

There was a loud flapping, farting sound as a man cut the mechanical prostitute in half with an axe—but when the bucket fell off its head, they realized it really hadn't been mechanical at all.

We were trying to creep away, but then the crowd turned back towards us—and they were angry. A tall man near the front held a massive, two-handed sword over his head like a crusader getting ready to charge.

"Right," I said. "So this is the part where we run away."

The mob chased us all through the city. First along the streets, but then when another crowd appeared ahead of us, we turned into an alley. All that way, we passed hundreds of crucified prostitutes—and sometimes the ones who were still alive would cheer us on a little.

During The Prostitute Genocide, the only way to be completely safe was to wear a shirt that said "prostitutes are retarded" in big red letters, having been approved by the official prostitute inspection/termination organization (PITO), but of course, neither of us were.

For a while, I'd experimented with chainmail—but no, I didn't like the way it jingled when I went places.

The National Union for the Termination of Prostitutes (NUTP) had taken over The City.

Nowhere was safe anymore.

Further down the alley, we ran into a huge fat guy dressed like a priest, carrying a flamethrower and cackling as beads of sweat dripped down his face. Behind us was a horde of children with sharpened silverware, trying to scoop our brains out and eat them.

If something like this had happened later in the book, Karen or the samurai would have come to save us, but it didn't, and we didn't have anyone to depend on.

We slowed down, turning back to look at the horde of screaming children, when suddenly there was a sound like a sack of meat splitting open.

The fat guy holding the flamethrower was dead, and his face was missing.

"Sorry!" called someone from above us.

He'd been hit by a falling anvil.

Later we were attacked by hordes of old women, wielding canes with poisoned spikes fastened onto the ends.

They almost got us, except we found a door on one side of the alley, and they must just have gone past it.

We entered a low room, filled with smoke. From ahead I could hear a loud crowd of people. Cement walls, covered with grime. Mathew and I did our best not to touch them, because they were dirty.

Eventually, the hall opened into a big open area with a bunch of people in it. There was some kind of gladiator match going on, except all of the fighters were dressed up as reality TV stars or ex-presidents.

We tried to slip towards a door on the other side.

We didn't fit in, it was obvious.

From beneath their sunglasses, two scary guys grabbed us and dragged us to a far corner of the room. On a big chair was sitting a very evil man.

He had eyes like a cat and he looked at us like dead animals.

"Is this them?" he asked.

Our captors grunted.

The evil man waved them away.

"Well," he said, crossing his hands into an X. "What do we have here?"

"My name is Mathew," Mathew said. "I'm innocent."

He was sort of shaking. The effect did not make him look very cool.

I was thinking of giving Mathew a chance to say something else, except just then he pissed his pants, and it really ruined the moment.

I can't believe it actually happened, but a trapdoor opened up beneath our feet, and we fell.

It was dark where we landed, and the smell was awful. On the ground were many, many bones, human bones, some with parts of the flesh left on them, but not many.

Mathew and I stood up. The ground was so damp that it was almost mud. It had gotten all over our clothes where we landed.

One side of Mathew's face was covered in shit. He tried to clean it off, but it didn't do any good.

"I can't take this." He kneeled down and pressed both hands against his face. "This is just too much."

"The corpses are a nice touch though," I added.

"WHY DO THEY HAVE A DEATHPIT?"

Mathew retched once, like he was going to vomit, but then he just sighed.

"Things this stupid shouldn't be allowed to happen," he said.

"I guess that's life. You can always depend on it to be more ridiculous than you expect."

I didn't blame him about the retching. The smell was

really getting to me.

But worse: on the far wall, I noticed the indented lines of a gate. It was a big gate, probably ten feet tall—like behind it was a monster, a real monster, a dangerous one.

"Do you see that?" I asked.

"I don't know. I hear something."

"You're right."

A kind of creaking sound, a churning of gears somewhere above us.

The gate was beginning to rise.

"Oh shit," Mathew said. "Oh shit. Oh fuck."

"Calm down, man," I said. "It's sort of derivative for there to be that much swearing in one paragraph. It's holding down the narrative."

"I don't care!"

The door was going higher, except it moved really, really slowly.

From behind it I could hear the low churning of some hideous beast, and a deep shuffle.

Whenever the monster moved, parts of it brushed along the ground.

It was chewing on the bones of small children.

"I want to be a baby again," Mathew said. "I want to be reincarnated as a grasshopper."

The door was more open now than it had been before.

The growl was getting louder, a sense of some beast coming inevitably closer.

Mathew began to laugh.

"If my sister was here," he said, "she would save us."

"When we get out," I said, "you should introduce me to her."

"No." He paused. "No, you really don't want to meet her."

"Oh," I said. "Ok."

In front of us there was a clank as the gate stopped moving. Then it just sort of hung there.

"I guess this is it," Mathew said.

"Everybody dies in the end," I said. "Everyone gets eaten by something."

A huge shadow lurked in the darkness. It came forward, tossing aside or crushing the remains of bone.

In front of us, there was a gigantic guinea pig, and it was hungry.

This is where all of my battle scars come from. Trust me, it doesn't sound quite as impressive as it is.

This is how we managed to get out:

Beyond the gate, where the guinea pig had been locked, there was a door with a stairway beyond it, where people came down in order to feed it—except, I guess, it had been left unlocked.

The guinea pig hadn't been able to get out on its own because it didn't have thumbs.

But we did.

I actually feel kind of bad about what happened afterwards. After Mathew and I ran up the stairs, the guinea pig came up behind us and killed almost everyone in the room. It swallowed the very evil man whole.

After that, it got outside and went on a rampage. Then it managed to kill every member of NUTP in The City.

.

I still kind of like guinea pigs, to be honest.

Where the darkness is

I was spending time with Karen in public, which was always sort of dangerous. She could be nice sometimes, for a little while, when she wanted to, if she was feeling merciful, but that wasn't often, even if sometimes it really happened, I swear.

While we were walking, she took my arm and held it against her. The feel of her body in clothes made me think of her without them.

She would destroy me.

"What are you thinking about?" she asked.

"You know. Stuff."

"Are you sure? I followed your eyes and they were stuck in the ceiling. When you gaze distant places like that and then answer evasively, I know you're thinking about something you don't want me to know."

"Wow," I said. "Very perceptive."

She smiled. "Right?"

"I still don't want to tell you, though."

"Why?"

"It's personal."

"I get it," she said. "You're thinking about sex."

"Again. Very perceptive."

"That's what I'm thinking about right now, too."

"Hmm. Interesting."

She laid her head on my shoulder and curled her arm across my chest.

She did not smell like a murderer.

"You know," she said, "sometimes it makes me sad. Because of who I am, people get hesitant about things, you know?"

"Yeah." I nodded. "I'm a little hesitant right now."

"You see? That's the way things always are for me, because of myself. I'm not sure what to do about it."

"I don't know." Without even meaning to, I was running my hands through her hair. "I wish I had some advice."

"Could you do me a favor?" she asked. "Find someone to love me, just for a while. Everyone needs to feel loved, sometimes."

"I don't know anyone. I don't know anyone, other than myself."

She curled against me, almost so that I was holding her up. But no, a better thing to say would be that she was floating. She hung suspended in the air because of her own weight.

"Please?"

"The problem isn't you," I said, "it's me."

"I'll be nice." She pressed her face against my neck. "I promise."

"I mean, I guess," I said. "It's not like I don't want to."

"That's good," she said, and grabbed me a little tighter.

"What are you doing?" she asked.

"Your hair," I said. "It's really soft."

She had brown hair. I don't know if I've mentioned that yet. Or maybe "auburn." I still have no idea what the difference between them is.

I pulled it to the side, and leaned down to kiss right above her ear.

"That tickles," she said.

"Oh. I'm sorry."

"No. Do it again. It feels nice."

"I think this makes me happy. I'm not sure, but I think it does."

She turned to face me, and I'm not sure where we were.

"Wait," I said. "What are you thinking about?"

"When we put our faces like this, in a line, they fit together."

"That's because we're human," I said. "It's the way we're shaped."

"Our lips," she whispered. "Our lips."

"We both have them."

"Definitely."

She touched them against mine, and they were soft too.

"I've never seen you like this before," I said.

"I'm not always like I always am. I thought you should know."

"You're cute. I don't think I ever told you how pretty I thought you were."

"Should I thank you? What do you think?"

"No," I said. "You don't need to."

"You make me feel good. I always knew that if we did something like this you would make me feel good."

I kissed her again.

"Are you serious?" Mathew asked.

We were playing ping pong. Yes, ping pong, because it's awesome.

"I know," I said. "Afterwards, I was sort of surprised."

"I don't know if you'll be safe."

"It doesn't feel like a mistake. I'm not sure."

Mathew hit the ball really hard, so that it flew over my shoulder to the other side of the room. He wiped a few beads of sweat off his face.

"I don't know," I said. "When I think of us, I think of a star, and then I think of that star falling out of the sky. It will catch on fire but then eventually disintegrate."

"So you think most likely she'll murder you and then bury you beneath a garden full of radishes?"

I nodded. "Something like that."

Because of the situation, Michelle and I decided that, for both of our safeties, it would probably be better if we stopped watching pornography together.

This was not an easy decision. Michelle cried a little. I smashed my face into the wall.

We said it wouldn't, but it would obviously put strain on our relationship.

"I'm sorry," I said.

"No. I understand."

"I'm not sure if I know why it happened. It just felt right, I don't know."

"Don't worry," she said, "I know what you mean."

We were sitting in my apartment like always, but then suddenly it didn't feel the same.

Karen and I were eating ice cream. I like ice cream because it's cold, and because of the flavor in it. It made my mouth cold, even if the day was warm.

Contrast.

"You know what I've been thinking about recently?" she asked. "Clowns. Really, they aren't very scary. They aren't very scary at all."

"I didn't know you were scared of anything."

"That's not true. There are things that frighten me."

"Like what?"

"Well, I've never screamed when I saw a spider, but sometimes I think about things, like, the way people behave and stuff, or the future, and it makes me hurt in my chest a little, inside. I think that's what fear feels like."

"I don't know," I said. "For me, fear is what happens when I look too long at the future, or at myself, and I realize that even when things feel safe, that's only the world as I imagine it, rather than how it really is. Fear is the moment when you realize something can be lost. It's like knowing, in a second, you're going to be eaten by a monster—it'll destroy you and nothing will be left, nothing meaningful or recognizable. But monsters eat a lot of things, not just people."

I was watching her mouth as she ate.

"Sometimes," she said, "I can tell why you're an author. You say poignant things sometimes."

"I don't think so," I said. "I haven't written anything in forever. And when I do, it's awful."

"That's your spirit of artistic angst. It radiates from you in waves."

"Right."

We were sitting beneath an umbrella in the sun. The umbrella was beneath the sun, not us.

It made the street a place of light. I could see all the people's feet walking on it.

Because we were looking at people, some guy must have thought we were interested in him. He came over to us and started talking to Karen.

Later, once the ambulances had left, I noticed someone out of the corner of my eye, even if I could hardly recognize him.

"Hey," I said, "isn't that Siguard? He's waving at us."

"Oh, yeah," she said. "That's him."

"What's wrong? He doesn't look the same."

"Well, remember after last time, when I beat him up for killing people?"

"I remember."

"It didn't stop him. Sort of randomly, I was walking home when, along the side street, I noticed he was mincing up a little girl. In order to stop him, I broke his face. I don't think he has any teeth anymore."

"Well shit."

"Do you think I did too much?"

"No, it's not that, he deserved it."

"He's coming this way. I sort of want to ignore him."

"Me too."

Siguard kept waving at us, calling out through many gurgled breaths. People gave him weird looks and spat whatever they were eating out of their mouths, because he was disgusting.

His face looked like a rock that had been hit far too many times with a hammer.

"Hi guys," he said.

"You can still talk?" I asked.

He nodded—crookedly. "I just got a new set of teeth! Isn't that exciting?"

"No," I told him. "Not really."

He shook both hands in front of himself. "Don't worry. I'm cured. Really."

"I don't believe you."

"If I catch you one more time," Karen added, "I'll rip your guts out through your mouth."

"Don't worry," he said, "I'm reformed. I swear."

After that, he reached into his pocket, and pulled out a miniature pipe.

"I've taken up crack," he explained. "Everything is all right now."

Karen and I were in her room. We lived in the same apartment complex, except on different floors, so it was basically similar to mine, except she had more furniture.

Even though Mathew's room was just one over, I'd never been in here. I hadn't been sure what to expect, but it was pretty much normal.

All of us were too poor to decorate. The intention, I think, had been for her to split the furniture her parents gave her with Mathew, but the only thing she let him keep was his bed.

I was sitting in a desk in the corner, doing homework. Karen was on the other side of the room, with her punching bag.

The sound of her attacking it gave me trouble focusing, but I didn't say anything. I just had to try finishing for a little while, so I could tell myself I'd made an effort.

When Karen was done, breathing hard, she came over behind me and wrapped her arms around my shoulders.

"What are you doing?" she asked, and bit me on the neck.

"Nothing," I said. "Just math. I really hate anything involving numbers."

"You're awful. If I was a teacher, I would say you have no future, and years from now you're going to die in a gutter with syphilis and hemorrhoids, while living on a diet of plastic wrappers, fermented rats, and moldy grass, with half of your limbs rotted off, and only one eye."

"You're too real. I can't take it."

"I'm just joking." She hugged me again, and kissed a trail along the side of my neck. "You don't have any sense of humor."

"I knew it was a joke," I said, and turned around so that we were facing each other. "Humor is the only way we have of disguising the emptiness and futility and darkness of this world, and sort of ignoring it for a little while. There's nothing to laugh at about that, no matter how funny it is."

She sat down on my lap, her legs on both sides of mine, and kissed me again. Her chest pressed against me and I was thinking about arousal.

I'm sure she knew, just from feeling.

"You're sweaty," I said.

"You like it," she said.

"Your skin tastes like salt," I said, tasting it. "And yeah, I do."

"Little girl," she said, pressing against me through my jeans, "what are you thinking about."

"I'm thinking that if you took advantage of me now, no matter how loud I screamed, no one would be able to hear us—except maybe Mathew, but all he would do is vomit and put on headphones, and he wouldn't be able to do anything about it."

"You wouldn't scream." She licked my face. "Of course you wouldn't."

"I was trying to be funny," I said.

"I thought I told you," she said, "you don't have any sense of humor."

"What's this?" I asked.

"What?" She sighed.

"Right here."

I held her left breast and kissed it, right above her heart. Her breasts were so big that they were actually heavy when I held them. That had never been my thing before, but I got used to it really quick.

"What do you mean?"

She thrust her stomach up against me, and it was smooth.

"There's a scar," I said, "right here," and touched it again, this time with my fingers. "It's really faint, but it's like a cut or something, about three or four inches wide."

She kept rubbing her pelvis against me. Each time, her breath got deeper.

"Don't," she said. "Don't ask me about that. It's not something I want to talk about."

"I understand. There are some things in this life we just have to forget."

"It's like you understand me."

"I don't know." My breath got heavier, until my voice was almost unrecognizable. "Hopefully I do."

Her hand closed over mine. She blew a strand of hair away from her face, and stared at me with her eyes.

"Don't say anything else," she said. "I don't want to think.

The way we moved, it felt like the world was stretching. She moaned.

The problem with my life is that even the good things are always ending and changing and going back to how they were before, how I remember them rather than how they ought to be. But in the end, I think maybe I need it: this sense of a solid foundation, of something dependable to return to. This is a strange world, full of scary things and scary people, and it's good to feel like no matter what happens, in the end, everything will be the same. Everything will be all right.

So, anyway, I was in class, on the second floor.

I stared at the teacher for a few seconds, then looked at the clock.

I flipped through my notebook a little. I looked back towards the clock.

My pencil fell off the desk, and I was glad for the chance to pick it up, because it gave me an excuse to move. Except then it fell off again.

To one side of the room, a bookshelf fell over on its side.

The teacher hit his face on the blackboard.

The entire room was shaking.

Red light shined in through the windows as outside, a gigantic volcano rose up from the ground, spewing lava and flying bits of rock. In the distance, they looked almost like birds, but no, there was nothing avian about them.

The teacher was bleeding. I think he probably had a concussion.

All of us were still in our seats. There was a sense like everyone was afraid to move, because moving would acknowledge the volcano.

Lightning struck, creating an explosion. The impact reverberated through the walls. The floor buckled and part of it collapsed.

After the first person fell out of their desk, no one was sitting still anymore.

The room was empty except a few stragglers who for some reason felt the need to put all of their things away before they left. There was the sound of rustling papers, and zippers being zipped.

The teacher was dead. He'd been trampled by everyone else as they left.

I got up and stepped across the floor. It wasn't too crooked, but it wasn't even, either.

I needed to find either Karen or the samurai.

The person I actually ran into wasn't either of those people, but I suppose he was better than nothing.

"Mathew," I said. "Do you have any idea what's going on?"

He shook his head. Sort of like me, he hadn't run away immediately. Our classes had both been on the second floor, just a few rooms away from each other.

"You know what we need to do, right?" I asked.

"Yeah, except I have no idea where they are. Do you know if the samurai still takes classes here?"

"They tried to kick him out," I said, "except whenever someone tried, he would kill them, so it never went well.

Most likely he's in a closet somewhere, meditating."

"I don't know where Karen is, either. But if there's something to kill, she might show up."

We kept walking in no particular direction. Red lights flashed continuously outside.

"Wait—" Mathew put his hand out. "Give me a second." He'd stopped outside a bathroom. "I need to take a piss. I don't want to ruin it like I did last time."

In the entrance hall, there was a huge fire. The fire was surrounded by a bunch of Japanese demons with red skin and *oni* masks, most of them naked except for their loin cloths. The demons were busy skewering the people who had run earlier and cooking them over the flames.

It was not a pleasant sight.

When we came down the stairs, all their eyes turned towards us, and I realized we were dead. I know they would have gotten us eventually, but standing there, about to be eaten, made me feel really stupid.

"Motherfucker," Mathew said. He would have pissed his pants, but since there was nothing there, he dropped to his knees and began to vomit.

He came up for air briefly, then knelt down to vomit again.

His vomit wrenched and splashed as it hit the floor.

"Stop that," I said. "You're freaking me out, man."

The demons were closing in. One of them scratched his head with a painfully huge finger. Another's loin cloth had come unfastened, revealing hideously furred genitals.

Mathew had vomited so much that one of the demons tripped on it, which startled all the others.

That gave us a chance to run, so I grabbed Mathew and dragged him back down the hallway. He left a slippery trail at our back, so maybe it would slow a few of them down.

The demons didn't seem to be very smart, but they were really strong. If we could get out of their sight, maybe they would forget about us.

Mathew choked. While we ran, the vomit got stuck in his mouth halfway, behind his throat.

A little around the corner was the door to a closet. I threw Mathew inside, then I went in too.

Fortunately for me, he couldn't throw up anymore, and now all he did was make choked gagging sounds, like a dying rodent, that had been shot, in a vital organ, with a high caliber rifle.

Mathew shivered a little and held both hands against his chest.

We heard loud crashing sounds from outside the door, and it seemed like any second now they would break it down. But then everything went silent, and when I looked out again, all of the demons were dead. The samurai stood above the bodies, holding his sword, his clothes all covered in blood.

"Mathew." I shook his body, which had gone limp. "We're saved, wake up."

A trail of brown liquid leaked from the corner of Mathew's lips.

"Right," I said. "Maybe I'll just leave you here for a while."

When I looked back into the hallway, the samurai had left as well.

But there was a girl standing there, and it was Karen. I can hardly explain how glad I was to see her.

"Do you know where Michelle is?" she said.

"It was just me and Mathew," I said. "Except Mathew is incapacitated." I pointed. She held her nose and grimaced. "Maybe he'll get better if we leave him in the closet."

"Hideyoshi is looking for Michelle. There's nothing we can do."

"Are you sure?"

She nodded.

"Anyway," I said. "What are you doing here?"

"I wanted to come get you. Mathew I don't care about, but I needed to make sure that you were okay."

"I appreciate that."

It made me feel like I mattered, a little bit. It really did.

It wasn't safe to leave The School, so all we could do was go towards someplace where we might not be found, preferably with a lock.

The volcano was spewing rocks. Stony hail broke the windows all around us.

Upstairs, amber light drifted in the evening. Rivers of lava flowed across the landscape, with countless people drowning in them. The sky was full of burning embers.

"What's that sound?" she asked.

"What do you mean?"

"It's like… footsteps," she said. "Something dragging."

In front of us, there stood some being whose entire body was made of dark fire. Flame defined its hooks and sinews. Naked, except for a mask in place of its face.

What looked like fire might only have been darkness. It had no shape when the wind hit it.

"Wait," Karen said. "Wait, we can't."

"We can't stop," I said. "It'll burn us to death."

"I can't go." She pulled away.

She took a step away. Her entire body shook.

"What's going on?" I asked. "This isn't like you."

"There's only one thing I'm afraid of. There's only one thing."

The being took another step closer.

I grabbed Karen, ran down the hall, turned a corner, and went inside a classroom.

The door had a lock. I'm not sure if it would keep anything out, but it made me feel better, at least.

Karen was crying. I didn't know her eyes were capable of producing tears.

"I just realized," I said. "What's up with the samurai? It seems almost too convenient to have someone like that around when we're attacked by Japanese demons."

Karen had stopped crying. She wiped her eyes one last time.

"You don't know?" she asked.

"Know what?"

"Hideyoshi isn't from now. He's a samurai from ancient Japan, sent here by his evil demon nemesis, the Lord of Fire. This is the end of an epic conflict that has gone on for hundreds, maybe thousands of years."

"That's dumb," I said.

"Do you not believe me?"

"No, it's not that. It's just... life is full of the most ridiculous surprises, and none of them make sense. None of them make sense, ever."

She paused, creating a moment.

The moment stretched.

"Is something wrong?" I asked. "You're crying again, aren't you?"

"No. You're imagining it."

"Now you're lying to me." I moved a little closer. "What's wrong? When you lie to me, it hurts my feelings."

"Do you swear?" she asked. "Do you swear you'll believe me?"

"I will," I said. "I promise."

She told me the story, then, of when the demon came and took her heart. It happened when she was very, very young. Before Mathew was even born.

One day, she was playing alone in a room. She kept looking out the window because it was afternoon and the setting sun made the world beautiful. It cast shadows that carved their own image on the carpet, traced with subtle warmth.

She lay down on the ground and felt safe. She had no idea the person she had been until that day was about to die.

There was a man standing above her, or something like a man. In the center of his chest was a box with a mouth, like teeth, and in place of his face was a dark mask. When he spoke, his voice rustled the trees outside, making them frightening, because they moved in ways she'd never known existed.

Hello, he said, leaning down to put his hand against her cheek. She was very afraid. He must have told her his name, but she had no idea what it was.

The wind blew outside, through the window, and

became his breath, distant and imaginary.

I am here to take something from you. But do not worry.
He leaned down so she could look directly into his mask,
seeing no face behind it. *You will not miss it. You will not
even know that something in you is gone.*

She didn't say anything because her mouth didn't
work anymore. She tried to move her arms but they only
stayed against the ground.

Be still. This will only take a moment.

He reached down, his hand sickly angular with long
nails sharpened into claws, and inserted the fingers into
her chest, where a bright light began to shine.

He rummaged through her chest as if searching for a
toy in a bin, corroding everything he touched. It hurt in
ways she was still unable to describe.

Here. This is it.

He withdrew his hand, and clasped in it, she saw
something she hardly recognized. Her heart looked
different than she would ever understand a heart to look,
but he only held it in the light for a moment, before
taking off his mask, and inserted it into his face, where it
disappeared.

He took her hand and pressed it against the box in the
center of his chest.

*You see this? If ever you find me again, perhaps I will give
it back, but I do not think that is likely.*

She didn't say anything as the figure above her became
mist, and was gone. But she felt empty without her heart,
and she'd felt that way, ever since.

"Before that," Karen said, "I was a nice person, I swear."

"It's fine. I like you the way you are now."

"That's not enough for me. Feel this." She took my hand, and pressed it against her chest. "Can't you tell? I don't have a heartbeat. I'm not like normal people."

"I'm sorry. I don't know what to say."

"That's fine. I just thought you should know."

We'd been in here long enough that it was getting dark outside. It was a hideous night, because the sky was still on fire, but when you didn't look directly, it wasn't so bad.

"I wonder what happened to Mathew," I said. "We probably shouldn't have left him downstairs in that closet."

"He's okay. Or he's not. It doesn't matter."

"I'm more worried about Michelle."

"If anyone can save her, Hideyoshi will."

Karen looked at me and smiled.

"You know," she said, "in moments like this, I sort of like you a little."

The City had turned into a battlefield.

Cars were turned over on their side, splattered with people. All of the buildings had been knocked down. I had to be especially careful, because of the lava.

On the horizon the torso of some gigantic being jutted higher than any of the buildings, naked to the waist with nine immense arms. Its skin was red and it had lightning for eyes. It was the source of all fire.

Even at this distance, I could see the giant fighting the samurai. It swung its arms—huge, lumbering swings, whistling in the air as they passed. The samurai ran up the giant's chest and jumped to cut at its face. It reached up and almost got him, but at the last second, he jumped onto a nearby building.

The giant spat fire and roared. Then its skin flared so brightly I had to look away.

And no—I wasn't planning on going any closer.

Karen and I walked the other way along the street, but all that way, their battle shook the earth. The sky was red, and way too many things were on fire.

Before we left The School, we'd stopped by the closet

again, and it was all my fault. Mathew had choked to death on his own vomit.

"Don't worry," Karen said. "I don't blame you."

"Right," I said.

"Just think," she added. "He already died once. No one will miss him this time, so it's all right."

"I guess it isn't so bad."

Though of course, it was.

Just then, the battle at our backs grew louder. Buildings shook, and plumes of fire seared the sky.

"Wait," Karen said. "It's Michelle."

There didn't seem to be many demons in this direction, but there were still a few ahead of us. I'd grabbed a sword from one of the dead ones, but only Karen would be able to fight.

Michelle's screams got louder the closer we went.

Suddenly, Karen stopped.

"What's up?" I asked.

She was looking distant. Her eyes turned away from me.

"I'm sorry," she said. "I have to go."

"What? Why?"

"My heart. It's here. I can feel it."

"Wait. I'll come with you."

"No. You can't."

"Fuck," I said. "Fuck it. Why?"

She never answered. She was already beyond the rubble.

She found the demon, the same one, in a valley between two collapsed buildings, walls of debris rising to either side. His body was a black outline covered with blood. It was difficult to tell, but he might even have been smiling.

Well, he said. *I was waiting for you.*

"You said you would let me have it back."

He laughed.

I will. Except, I must tell you, in all likelihood, you will no longer want it.

"Why?"

Over these many years, the remnants of your heart have been corroded. If I give it back, it will change you.

"Give it to me."

She took a step closer.

If that is what you desire, I will not stop you, but you have been warned.

The mouth on his chest came open—a hole lined with many fangs, rimmed with the stunted formations of eyes. Karen put her hand inside and drew out a lump of blackness: sickly, corroded, spewing streams of green fluid.

You see? You cannot possibly want it back.

"I don't care," she said. "I don't care anymore."
The light that came from her heart was all black.

Michelle's head had been cut off. Two thin demons were playing catch with it in the middle of the street. I never found out what had happened to her body.

When they saw me, the demons turned and began to laugh. Then I stepped forward, and cut both of them in half.

I picked up Michelle's head, cradled it in my arms, lay down on the ground, and began to cry. A pool of blood spread out around me.

The blood was mine. I wouldn't be able to stand again.

I pressed my lips against Michelle's forehead. I could hardly see through my tears.

"This isn't right," I said. "This isn't how it's supposed to end."

"Don't worry," said her lips. "Everything will be all right soon."

"I thought—I thought this was supposed to be a funny story."

She was crying too. That was the truth of that moment, when we both saw each other's tears.

"I thought you didn't believe in comedy." she said.

"Isn't that what you told me?"

"Yeah," I said. "It's a lie. The problem comes like with all lies, when you start to believe it."

The truth was that I was holding Michelle's severed head and bleeding to death.

There was nothing funny about that. Nothing at all.

Stuff that happens when it is snowing outside (an interlude)

There was snow all over The City, and it was time to celebrate Christmas. I was almost tired of Christmas music, since it was so awful, but not quite.

Because I was the only one with a functioning video game console, we decided to have Christmas in my apartment. None of us have any other friends or lives so all we do is spend time with each other.

Mathew came over and he was wearing a red sweater. It had a picture of a reindeer on it. When he came closer, I noticed glitter on it. I would never wear something like that.

Karen got there a little after, and then Michelle. All of us were carrying presents. A present is a box with colored ribbons on it. We were not children, but that has never stopped anyone, anywhere, from acting like one.

Mathew was eating cookies and drinking coffee. All the food was mine again, but I guess I sympathized, because whenever he has something she wants Karen takes it from him.

Michelle asked, "You said you put up a Christmas tree, right?"

"Over there." I pointed. "It's sort of sitting in the

corner, on top of the table."

"It's like three inches tall," Karen said.

"Sorry. I did my best."

I should have known better than to turn around. Karen threw a fork, and if I hadn't ducked, it would have hit me right in the neck.

"So…" Michelle said, "how is everybody feeling today?"

"Cold," Mathew said.

Thus: the sweater.

"I've been thinking about capitalism," I said. "I've erected an altar to capitalism, so we can pay it tribute and stuff."

"What are you talking about?" Karen asked.

"I get it," Mathew said. "Christmas is our yearly celebration of consumerism and greed and corporate servitude. That sort of ruins it for me, though."

"Look very carefully," I said, "at the tree."

Everyone put their faces close and acted contemplative.

"That's… a twenty dollar bill, isn't it?"

"Indeed."

"So we should pray, right?" Mathew said.

"I was thinking we could wish for things," I said.

"I don't think…" Michelle paused. "I'm not sure if we're really celebrating Christmas anymore."

"For the record," I added, "if anyone takes the tree, I'll have to hurt them. It's like all the money I have left."

I wasn't sure when, but Karen had wandered away, because she didn't like listening to me talk. Especially when I was trying to make a point.

That was probably for the better. It still made me really uncomfortable to be around her.

All of us sat down on the ground beneath the twenty dollar tree. More Christmas music played in the background.

All of us had received two presents, with the exception of Michelle, who had three. Mathew hadn't gotten anything for Karen or I. He didn't mention it often, but he was still angry about us letting him choke to death on his own vomit.

"So," I said, "how do you want to do this? The best way would probably be to go around in a circle."

"Michelle can go first," Mathew said, "since she has the most."

"I'm fine with that."

Michelle opened Mathew's present first. It was one of his favorites: a figurine of a girl killing trout with a machete. Naked.

"Oh," she said. "This is... nice."

The funny thing, I think, is that she never even took it out of the box.

I'd bought Karen a mallet from a hardware store, since it seemed fitting.

"Aww," she said. "That's very considerate of you."

"Thanks," I said. "I'm glad you like it."

The problem was that as soon as she stopped cradling the mallet against her chest, she started doing practice swings. Everyone moved away but there still wasn't much space in the room. It wouldn't be long before she was breaking stuff.

Mathew was next; he opened his present from Karen first. He tore off the wrapping paper, opened the box, and inside, there was a massive purple dildo.

"Cute," he said. "Maybe I'll put it on a shelf somewhere."

"You'll find a use for it." Karen narrowed her eyes. "You'd better."

I opened my present and there was a dildo in it too.

"See?" Karen said. "You guys can have sword fights. It'll be great."

"Sure," I said, putting the lid back on. "Thanks."

Michelle opened her present from Karen and it was a sweater.

The circle came back around to Mathew and he opened his present from Michelle. Inside, there was another dildo.

"You too?"

"I'm sorry." Michelled blushed. "I just thought... I don't know, it seemed right for you. I didn't mean to get you the same thing as Karen."

The dildo was bright pink, so big you could have killed a squirrel with it.

I picked up my present from Michelle, but I already knew what would be inside.

Mathew and I tossed our presents someplace. I sort of wished I hadn't been given anything at all.

"Eggnog," I said, "is the weirdest drink in the world. Isn't it weird? Why is it so weird?"

All of us were mildly drunk. I lay back and the couch felt very, very soft.

Michelle and Karen were on the other side of the room, talking about something only interesting to girls. I wasn't sure what, because as soon as I tried listening, I lost my ability to pay attention.

All the cookies were gone. Mathew's stomach growled.

I almost felt happy. I'm not sure if that was the best word to describe it, but at least, I felt less sad than I usually do. I looked up at the ceiling and wondered why I felt almost like I was going to cry.

"Are you all right, man?" Mathew asked. "I know she's even worse now than she was before."

"Don't worry. I'm over it. Besides—it ended better than I thought it would. At least this way she's back to being her true self, or something like that."

"No." Mathew shook his head. "She lost her heart a

long time ago, and she won't get it back. I'm not sure what happened, but this isn't her at all."

I was trying to be optimistic, but it was just a waste of time.

"Nothing makes sense," he said. "It's kind of sad, really. The only light this world has doesn't illuminate anything. All it does is shine brighter, so we have to pay attention to the things we don't want to see."

I wish he wouldn't be so profound, by accident.

Outside, in the center of the street, the aliens were celebrating Christmas too. They had erected a holographic Christmas tree—really tall, shining brightly with lots of different colors—and were passing out presents to all the little boys and girls.

They had more Christmas spirit than any of us.

In the distance, beyond them, a gigantic guinea pig was destroying The City.

It was still Christmas, though, so I didn't worry about it.

Onto the dust, the waves: a bridge between
spaces, which aren't...

I should probably explain how we got to be out in the center of the ocean.

A huge wave came up, jostling aside pieces of planking and floorboards. There were seagulls feeding on the wreckage, and the wave disturbed them.

Nature can be so discourteous, sometimes.

I'm not sure how, but Mathew had managed to win four tickets for a super awesome vacation. He told me where a few times, and I said that was cool. After a few weeks I kind of wanted to murder him again.

Mathew and I were experiencing strains in our friendship at the time. He still hadn't gotten over the fact that I'd let him choke to death on his own vomit, and then left him in a closet to die; not to mention, he'd decided never to talk to Karen again, for various reasons, all of them obvious. The only person he still got along with was Michelle, but all they did was watch porn together, and that only goes so far.

Mathew decided that, instead of us, he would go on vacation with two porn stars and a maid (also a porn star, in disguise). Two of them flew in from across The City, and lived with him for a day. This was, most likely, the happiest he'd ever been.

Unfortunately, it was not to last. On the second day, all of his money disappeared, and so did they. I'm pretty sure only one of them managed to run. The other two turned up later that night in the morgue.

"You're terrible!" Mathew said. "I can't believe you."

Karen was whistling and checking her cellphone.

"Me?" she asked.

"This is too much. It's too much."

"Calm down," I said. "All things die in the end. All things move inevitably towards nothingness."

"I don't care." It surprised me to see Mathew so close to sobbing. His entire body was made of contained rage, thrusting impossible directions. "I just wanted to be happy, for a little while. She ruins everything for me. She is the thing wrong with this world."

A few feet away, Karen was sending a text message.

Mathew had also invited Michelle originally, but she'd turned him down, because she didn't want to travel anywhere with two porn stars. He'd taken it personally, from what I can tell.

I don't know. Sometimes he was a pretty dumb guy.

In the end Mathew did take us with him, but he wasn't happy about it.

"Seriously," he said, "don't fuck this up. This is important to me."

Karen was messing with her armrests.

"Of course," she said. "Who do you think I am?"

I sat next to Michelle. She had her hands folded over her lap, looking out the window. Mathew and Karen were somewhere in front of us.

"Hey," I asked. "Are you all right?"

"I suppose," Michelle said. "Why?"

"Well, it's just, over the last twenty pages or so, you've only had like six lines. You seem distant, somehow."

"I didn't mean to be like that. I've just had a lot on my mind. That's all."

"You can tell me, if you want. It might help."

"Maybe," she said.

"Do you feel like talking, or should I be quiet?"

"I just... I don't like this. I don't like how things have been."

"Yeah," I said. "It feels wrong. Like nothing is in its right place anymore."

Or maybe it never had been.

I've never felt like I knew Michelle very well. Partially because she didn't talk very much; but maybe it might be because she didn't trust me, that I wasn't quite the person I could have been—and, as we talked for a while on that plane, I regretted that, and thought I would try to fix it if I could. Not just me and Michelle, but Mathew and Karen too, because something was wrong and none of us knew how to fix it.

But it turned out, I never had a chance.

After about an hour, from further up the aisle, Mathew began to scream. I looked out between the seats and he was on his knees, crying.

"Why!!!!!" he yelled. *"Why do you have to do this to me? This is so unnecessary!"*

Karen stood above him, holding twin machine guns.

"Everyone!" she exclaimed. "Put your hands down. I'm taking this plane."

Mathew crawled beneath the seat and curled up in a ball.

"You're so awful," he sobbed. "I hate you."

One man a few rows over raised his hand.

"I'm sorry," he said. "I'd like to go to the bathroom. Is that all right?"

It was not all right.

Karen shot him, and he died.

Michelle and I slouched as far down as possible.
We were kind of embarrassed, to be honest.

I'm not sure what happened next, because I wasn't there, and I never got the chance to ask. Even my memory of it isn't very good, because of what happened afterwards.

Karen went into the cockpit. The pilot didn't see her because he was too busy flying the plane. Along the way, she'd incapacitated three stewardesses and a young boy, then gone back to kick the young boy in the face.

She put the gun against the back of the pilot's head. Most probably, he was surprised by the coldness of it against his skin.

"Take off your pants," she said. "I'm the one flying this plane now."

"I can't," he said. "It will put everyone onboard in danger." He pressed back against the seat. His brow quivered a little.

"Your pants," Karen said.

"What? Why?"

A moment of inaction, then Karen hit him in the face, twice, with the butt of the gun.

"Take them off," she said.

I feel sorry for the things that gun would do to his rectum.

A few minutes later, the plane crashed into the center of the ocean.

I woke up, and all of us were in the water.

The plane had broken in half, scattered into pieces, and everything was on fire.

Trails of smoke leaked up from the wreckage.

Someone a few feet away from me had been impaled on the corner of their cellphone.

"Michelle," I called. "Are you okay?"

A big airplane seat was floating nearby, and I grabbed onto it. Staying afloat had now become considerably less difficult.

I called her name again, but nobody answered.

A small family was drifting through a circle of stuffed animals. About thirty feet away, Karen had tied a lot of people together and was using them as a raft. The ones on bottom were having an especially bad time.

I found a golf club and began using it as a paddle, through the smoke and the debris.

A few feet in front of me, there was a foot sticking out of the water. The foot moved. For a second I thought the foot itself was haunted, until I realized it was just attached to a body.

I pulled the foot out of the water. It turned out to be

Mathew. His shirt had gotten caught on something.

Breathing hard and sputtering, he coughed a huge mouthful of water.

If I hadn't been there, he might have choked to death.

"Now I know what it feels like," he gasped, "to be a fish. I won't give you too many details, but it's not good."

"That sucks."

"When the plane crashed, I was still under the seat. That was a bad choice."

"It's no good regretting things you did in the past." I patted him on the back. "You have to move forward."

He coughed some more, and it sounded like his stomach was about to come out.

Not quite, but almost.

"When I find her again," Mathew said, "I'll kill her."

"I know. It's ridiculous."

"No," he said. "It's different this time. She did this just because she doesn't like me."

"I'm not sure if she can help it. She's basically possessed."

"I don't care. I'm going to kill her."

Mathew's breathing was finally coming back. He braced himself, just looking into the water.

"I know you don't like to talk about this," he said, "but when you were with her, how did you stand it?"

"It was nothing like this. She was nice to me, mostly."

Mathew shook his head. "I can't imagine."

"Yeah," I said. "Neither can I."

"You know," Mathew said, "I should probably tell you, I'm sorry for being angry at you for so long. Especially now that you've saved my life again, we're even."

"No," I said. "I'm sorry. It wasn't nice of me, to let you die like that."

"I understand. You didn't know, right?"

"Yeah, I didn't know."

"Karen is different though. She could have helped me."

"Well, there's no telling what she'll do."

"Right," he said.

We spent fifteen minutes searching for Michelle. Once, I saw blonde hair floating face down, except it was just someone else, so I put her back in the water.

The irony is that Karen had pulled Michelle out of the water a long time ago. How is it, I wondered, that Karen was able to do more good than me, when she was evil and possessed by something more evil still?

It didn't make any sense. I wish more things would make sense in this life.

Every few minutes, other people would try climbing up onto Karen's raft, but whenever they did, she would push them off.

"Huh?" she said, looking down at us. "Oh. It's you."

"Won't you let us on?" I asked. "Please?"

Someone drowned a few feet away, and it was oddly satisfying.

"You," she said, meaning me, "can get on. But you," meaning Mathew, "can't."

"But I'm your brother!"

"Family," she said, "means nothing to me."

"You're terrible," he said. "You're the worst."

I climbed up onto the raft and sat down. It was weird, because I was standing on top of someone else's face. I would have liked to say something, but I'm sure Karen would have thrown me off.

Michelle was sitting a few feet away. Her hair was wet and so were her clothes. I could see the shape of her body a little, and it made me forget about where we were, and start thinking about other things.

Mathew was still struggling in the water.

"When we get back home," he said, "I'll be your slave for like two weeks."

Karen finally let him on when they settled at six months.

But then she punched him once, in the face—just for fun—and again in the windpipe, to see him choke.

He sputtered and fell. Breath would not enter him.

I was becoming far too accustomed to seeing him cry.

I sat on the raft for a while before I realized there was one more person with us. He was difficult to notice, because he didn't make a sound, but yes—that was the samurai on the far corner, meditating.

"Holy shit," I said. "What are you doing here?"

He opened his eyes. "I was on a journey to return to my homeland," he said. "Now that I have finally defeated the Lord of Fire, there is no purpose to my remaining in your City."

"Umm," I said. "That's not where we were going. The plane wasn't headed for Japan."

"What?" His eyes opened much wider, with shock. "How could this be?"

. . .

. . .

He must have gotten on the wrong flight.

The raft drifted away from the wreckage of the plane. Karen didn't let anyone else on, and eventually they stopped following, so it was just us like always, the same group of people, except in the ocean.

Michelle still wasn't talking much. Karen stood poised at the head of the raft, both feet directly on someone's face.

Her eyes scanned the horizon. She produced a telescope from somewhere and pointed it out over the water.

"She must have been planning this," Mathew said. "There's no way she would have brought a telescope otherwise."

"I think you hurt her feelings," I said, "by not inviting her originally. This is her way of getting revenge."

"That's not fair, and it doesn't make sense. I won't forgive her for this."

"Don't worry. I know."

Michelle still wouldn't talk. Her eyes were caught in the waves, drifting up and down with them.

"Sometimes," Mathew said. "I wish our lives were more normal, you know?"

"It's sort of like you said," I told him. "I think we just have really bad luck."

Karen let out a cry of something like happiness. She made the telescope smaller and put it back wherever it had come from.

"There's a ship," she said, "on the horizon!"

"Awesome!" I said. "We're saved."

The whole time, Mathew was inching further away. He didn't want to be by her.

"It'll be nice to get out of these clothes," I said. "They have salt all dried over them."

"I really hate cramped spaces," Mathew said. "And the floor of this thing is sort of uneven."

"They've spotted us!" Karen said. "They're coming closer."

It took a while for us to see them, but yes, eventually a small dot appeared over the line of the ocean.

It was interesting, because the ship looked really old, and the whole thing was made of wood. There was a statue of a naked woman on the front, and big, wide sails.

It was only when I looked more carefully that I realized something was wrong.

"Well shit," I said.

"What?" Mathew asked.

"Look at the flag," I told him. "Can't you tell?"

"Not really. Is there something wrong?"

"Yeah," I said. "It's a fucking *pirate* ship."

They brought us on board like pieces of meat—leering old men looking strangely like pirates should look, wearing torn up clothes and scabbards with swords in them, most of them bearded, and way too many with eye patches.

They crowded us on deck and formed a circle around us. I'm not sure what they did with the raft.

The thing that bothered me was their complete lack of hygiene. They smelled awful, all of them, and every once in a while some of them would just piss onto the floorboards.

"*Oi!*" said one. "*What do we have here...?*"

They were ogling Mathew. One of them reached out to grab him, and he pulled away.

"*I'm gonna fuck that arse till it bleeds like a goat.*"

"*Aye, till it bleeds like a goat.*"

There were so many I could hardly even tell them apart from each other.

"*Look at that one there!*" Meaning me, I think. "*He looks afraid.*"

"*I'll give him something to be afraid of, lads,*" cawed another. "*Me cock, in his eyehole.*"

It was really weird. They all seemed to have perfect pirate accents.

"*Oi, but there's girls too. What should we do with them?*"

"*They can walk the plank. We don't need no women on this ship.*"

"*Feed them to the sharks! Feed them to the sharks!*"

"*And what about this one? The slanty eyed fellow, with his hair tied back all funny.*"

"*We'll pickle his corpse, and put it on deck as a decoration!*"

They liked that idea quite a bit.

I didn't like the idea of being tossed into the ocean. Mathew looked particularly afraid, but it wasn't like normal. There was something building beneath the surface. There was anger in him, and eventually it would destroy something.

Karen stepped forward. She had the telescope again, except something made it look like a weapon now.

"I'm sorry to tell you," she said, "but I'll be taking this ship. We can do this the easy way, or the hard way."

One of the pirates scratched the side of his head. Another blew his nose with one hand.

"I *said*," she told them, "I'm taking this ship, and there's nothing you can do about it."

Finally, all of them broke out into laughter. One swaggered forward with a pirate walk. He stood out from the others because he had both a hooked hand and a pegleg.

"I like you, lassie," he chuckled. "You've got spirit. My name is Redbeard, and this is me ship. I've changed my mind from before. I'll be taking ye as me mistress." He tapped his pegleg on the ground and hooted. "We'll be having *much* fun tonight."

They all laughed, and a few of them broke into a pirate song. They still smelled really bad.

Redbeard leered. He reached out towards Karen with a big grin.

"I wouldn't do that if I was you," Mathew said.

"What, mate?" he asked. "This?"

I'm sure he didn't even see it coming.

This is when I learned what it looks like to see a girl destroy a pirate's face.

"Oi!!!!!" Redbeard screamed. "Oi!!!!!! You'll puncture me colon, you will! Me co-lon!"

Around them, a bunch of pirates were ruptured and beat up. Their bones creaked like old wood that had already been broken. They moaned and said "argh" every few seconds.

Karen had taken off Redbeard's pegleg, attached it to her pelvis, and was fucking him with it. Every few seconds he would scream. Huge tears came out from his eyes, and spit flew from his lips, streaming down to mingle with his beard—which was just brown, by the way.

"Call me daddy!" Karen screamed. "Call me your fucking daddy!"

"Oi!!! The pain! You'll rupture me digestive track! I'll be shitting wrong for a year!"

"Call me," she said, speeding up, "your fucking *daddy*."

Redbeard's face was about to pop. Some of his teeth were chipped, and they were so yellow a few of them might fall out soon.

Pirate dental hygiene was obviously not very good.

Later, Redbeard gathered up his pants (maybe a pirate would call them "trousers?"), and did his best to get the tears out of his eyes. All the pirates who were still conscious crowded around him.

"We'll be taking them back to land, mates. Immediately."

He was standing on one leg. Karen held his peg in one hand, and kept poking him in the mouth with it.

"We set out," Redbeard gagged, "this very minute. Until then, we'll entertain them the best we can, won't we?"

Karen stopped and grinned. Then she tossed his peg out over the side of the ship.

"Oi! That's me leg!"

"You can go get it, right? What kind of pirate can't swim?"

"I've... got replacements. I'd rather not wear it again, anyway, to be honest."

About half of the crew went away to their quarters or maybe the sick bay. The rest stayed on deck, looking sort of like they'd just come from a battle.

"*What say we break out the ale, mates?*" exclaimed one.

A rousing cheer rang out, and huge kegs appeared. I found out later they'd started a Karen fan-club, because she was the biggest badass they'd ever seen.

Yes, I know it sounds really strange, but this is how we ended up getting drunk with a bunch of pirates.

Everyone really broke into the ale. I've never seen anyone who could drink like these pirates did—and Mathew tried to keep up, which was maybe a bad idea, but whatever.

I got the feeling they did this almost every day, whenever they didn't have somewhere to rape and pillage. They looked really dangerous, but since all they had was a few rusty muskets, I don't think much pillaging actually took place.

I spent most of that evening pirate-watching. It was very anthropological.

One came up to me and wrapped his arm around my shoulder. It was really hairy, and he smelled like a rancid ballsack, sweating in the summer. I pushed him away, and stumbled towards the railing.

A group over on the other side were playing some kind of drinking game. It entailed, basically, singing a song and drinking. Mathew was playing too, and getting his ass kicked. No one seemed to know what the rules were, so it was all right.

I have no idea where Karen went. To be honest, I really didn't want to know.

Michelle was the only other one not joining in.

At the front of the ship, there was a carving of a naked woman, where nobody was drinking. Here, it was completely dark.

I almost couldn't see her, even if I knew she was there. She'd curled up with her arms around her knees.

"Are you all right?" I asked.

"Maybe," she said. "It's just… a lot's happened, you know."

"Yeah, I know."

"I don't feel right. I want to go home."

"Me too. I don't like it here."

I leaned my head on her shoulder. Even though there was salt in it, her hair was soft, and it smelled good. The skin of her neck was smooth.

"I have a feeling," she said, "everything is going to get worse before it gets better."

"That's fine. For now, all we can do is sit here, while there's still time."

I kissed her once on the cheek, and both of us stopped being awake, for a little while.

When we woke up, it was storming.

The entire sky was full of lightning. Like, all of it—a gigantic net of burning energy, in place of the clouds. Gargantuan waves, like rolling boulders, crashed onto the deck of the ship. The wind blew so hard it was impossible to stand up straight.

"Michelle," I said, "are you all right?"

She nodded. Both of us kneeled down, doing our best to keep away from the wind. We'd have to cross all the deck in order to get inside.

The worst part is that the sails were still up. Some of the pirates were trying to fix everything, but they were too drunk. Most of them could hardly even stand.

"Look at that!" Michelle shouted directly into my ear, muted by thunder.

"What?"

"Up there! It looks almost like someone's flying."

I looked closely, and yeah, she was right—hanging onto the end of a rope maybe attached to the mast, almost fifty feet over the deck of the ship, someone was being flung around by the wind. Because of the dark, I couldn't tell for a second that it was Mathew, screaming and vomiting at the same time.

I have no idea how he got up there, but it must have been pretty interesting.

Michelle and I kept going across the deck. We held onto each other, hopefully to make sure we didn't get separated.

It didn't work.

My face was pressed into the sand, and some of it had gotten into my eyes. Not to mention, I'd been sleeping in a really weird position, and my neck hurt. I'd gotten used to hearing waves, but these were different, somehow.

The beach was strewn with bits and pieces of wreckage, but otherwise it was empty. A line of trees started about fifty feet up, and went back I'm not sure how far. At least the sky was clear, but I really didn't care about the weather.

I sat up, and everything about me felt sore.

I would have expected at least one pirate to wash up nearby, but there were no pirates.

There weren't even any footprints in the sand.

In a sense, being alone like this—for the first time in my life, really, since I'd never left The City before—ought to have been liberating, but really all it did was make me feel small.

I walked up the beach and was glad when I came across Mathew. He'd been buried head-first in the sand, like an arrow shot from a bow or something, but it didn't take too long to dig him out.

He would be spitting dirt all day.

"I'm glad you're all right, man. I saw you up there and I wasn't sure."

"It was awful." He winced. "And to make it worse, I have a hangover. A really bad one."

"That sucks."

He was too sick to move, so we stayed in the same place for almost half an hour.

It was really convenient, because this way, Karen, Michelle, and the samurai found us, and we didn't even have to look.

"Hey," I said. "I'm glad you guys are all right."

Karen smiled. To be honest, I hadn't been worried about her at all.

"So," Mathew said, "have you found anyone else on the island? Is there anything here?"

"Not that we can tell," Karen said. "There's just trees, lots and lots of trees. And leaves. And dirt."

"Oh," I said. "I guess that's how islands are."

We sat down on the sand facing out towards the ocean. I couldn't be sure what time it was, because my cell phone was gone, but it might have been around noon.

This wasn't exactly a tropical island. That was nice during the day, because the air right now was warm and comfortable and stuff, but at night it would get really cold.

"Well then," Mathew said.

Karen had walked away while we were talking. She took a lump out of her pocket and tossed it into the bushes.

The leaves moved, like there was something behind them, but most likely I imagined it.

"Karen," I said. "Do you have any ideas?"

The samurai was meditating nearby. He had yet to say

a word during the conversation.

He didn't reply, and neither did Karen.

"The first thing we'll want to deal with," I said, "is food. How are you guys feeling? Do you have anything to eat?"

"Hmm." Mathew rummaged through his pockets and pulled out a candy bar. "I think this is it."

"Do not worry," said the samurai. "I can survive for weeks on a single grain of rice. I will fend for myself."

"Well," I said, "good to know someone's got it taken care of, at least."

Once Karen had gone somewhere else, I went behind the bushes and saw Redbeard tied up with a gag over his mouth.

He was struggling with his bonds, but it didn't do any good. I'm not sure where Karen had gotten the rope to tie him up with.

"Oh," I said. "It's just you."

"Mmm!" he said. "Mmm!"

"You want me to take this thing off your mouth?"

"Mmm!"

I did take the gag out of his mouth, eventually. I think he had to go to the bathroom too, but there are some things you just don't help a pirate with.

"Oi!" he said. "It was terrible, mate, the things that lass did to me."

"Yeah, I noticed."

"If you untie me, I promise I'll help ye get off this island. Pirate's honor."

"Ehh, I think I'll have to pass."

"You aren't going to leave me here, are ye? That would be too cruel."

"Just yesterday," I pointed out, "someone from your crew was talking about sticking their penis in my eye."

"He was just joking," scoffed Redbeard, "the old chap. All in good fun, all in good fun."

I took a step back, and looked around. Karen had hidden him about twenty steps back beneath the trees. Little slivers of light came through, but it was much darker here than on the beach.

"Anyway," I said, "I'm going to have to leave you here, but I wish you the best, and stuff. It's your own fault—if you hadn't originally intended to kill me, I would have been much nicer."

"It's all in the past, isn't it?"

"Not too far in the past. This was hardly even a day ago."

"Argh. God damn ye."

"It's not personal. I just don't think it would be a good idea to let you go. What would you do in this situation?"

"I would kill ye," he spat, "and eat ye."

"See?"

He sort of hunched his shoulders, and sulked a little.

"At the very least," he said, "could ye bring me some food? The lass's been tossing me scraps of dead animals, but I admit, I'm not brave enough to eat them."

"I'll do my best."

He gave me a gruff "Thanks" and looked down. The forest moved around us, but I tried not to pay attention to it.

"Only yesterday," Redbeard said gruffly, "I thought myself a man of distinction. I had me ship, me crew, and me honor. So quickly, I lost all of these things. I cannae even take a shit without horrible pain."

"Well," I said. "So it goes."

I went back onto the beach and Michelle was still gone. Karen had left to go hunting. The samurai hadn't moved. Mathew was throwing small rocks out into the ocean.

I sat down and looked at the sky. Then I looked at the waves. There weren't any patterns in them, so I wasn't very interested.

After a while, it started getting dark. I fell asleep at least once. Michelle came back, and I went to go sit next to her. Mathew had gathered a bunch of sticks to try making a fire. Karen was still out hunting.

Mathew got a bunch of leaves and tossed them on as well. He had a lighter, but it was half out already, so after this we would have to find some other way to start a fire.

Mathew had never been a boy scout.

Eventually, after he'd given up from failing so many times, we all sat watching as the sky became a pattern, leading onto darkness. I have no idea what we felt. Resignation, probably, that we were going to die here and there was nothing we could do about it. That's a hard feeling to describe.

There was a rustle from behind us and Karen came out through the trees, carrying a dead boar over her shoulders. She was covered in blood, and her hair was all wild.

She hefted the thing and tossed it onto the ground. It landed heavily and just sort of sat there, like a dolphin in a coma.

"Dinner," she said.

"It's no good," Mathew said. "I was trying to start a fire earlier, but I wasn't able to."

"You," she said, "are pathetic."

Karen backhanded him in the face and set off towards the forest. She came back carrying two huge logs and quite a few sticks.

Mathew was still nursing his wound. One side of his face had started to swell up.

"See?" She tossed the logs onto the pile he'd made. "This is how you do it."

Taking a deep breath, she paused, and spat a thin stream of flame towards the kindling. The fire caught, and crackling filled the air, creating a plume of smoke.

Mathew screamed and crawled backwards on the ground.

"What?" he trailed off. "There's no way...."

"You're helpless without me," Karen said.

We managed to cook the boar after stripping off the skin and guts, and jabbing a stick up its asshole. Mathew vomited twice, and I got the feeling my hands would never be clean again. Only Michelle was cool about it.

The whole time, Karen stood over our shoulders. She held a spear she'd sharpened from one of the trees. Her clothes were torn to allow her better mobility, her shirt cut off beneath her breasts. She licked her lips and grinned.

The results could have been better, but they weren't bad. As the boar cooked—part of it, since it was too big to fit over the fire; we didn't know what to do with the rest—we all sat around the fire and talked. Things almost felt normal, which was nice.

The only problem is that Mathew was never able to eat. As soon as he tried, Karen smacked the food out of his hand.

"Who said that *you* could have any?"

"Umm," he said.

I could tell that, beneath the surface, he was furious.

"Around here," she said, "I'm the boss. And I didn't give you permission to eat."

"You can't be serious?"

"We need to conserve our supplies, for the future."

"There's so much! That doesn't make any sense."

She hit him in the face, and he bled.

At first it seemed like a joke, but she never did let him eat.

It got even later, until no light remained in the sky. Michelle and I went as far away from Karen as possible, and Mathew went over somewhere to pound a rock against the sand, so only the samurai stayed with Karen around the fire.

I didn't mention it, but all night, he'd been drinking salt water as if it were tea, with the same motions and gestures and everything, which I thought was pretty cool.

It was only then I realized I'd never given any food to Redbeard. Karen had been guarding Mathew all night, so I never had the chance to feed him, but I think she'd forgotten about the pirate.

I got up and walked towards the forest. I hoped she would think I was leaving to piss or something. At first I thought I'd gotten the spot wrong—but no, he just wasn't there.

Before I left, even though it was dark, I saw a splotch of blood on the ground.

"You guys!" I said. "It's Redbeard, he's gone!"

Except, suddenly, I wasn't worried about that anymore.

Karen was standing above Mathew, holding a rock.

One side of the stone was covered in blood, and Mathew's skull was caved in, so that the brains tumbled out. She looked at me and her eyes glowed red.

I could see them, even in the darkness.

"Michelle," I whispered. "Hey, wake up, we have to go."

"What?" she asked, opening her eyes. "Why?"

"It's Karen." It was strange, knowing what was still happening like twenty feet away. "She killed Mathew, and I think she's... eating him."

Michelle opened her eyes. Then she turned, and saw what I'd seen, and she was completely awake.

I could hear a churning, thrashing sound, even from so far away—like fatty fibers tearing, threads being stretched thin—and there was a heavy weight in my throat.

"Yeah," Michelle said. "You're right, we should go."

We ran a way down the beach, both of us breathing hard, and fortunately Karen either hadn't seen us go, or didn't want to follow.

"Thanks for waking me up," Michelle said. "It was really considerate of you."

"No problem," I said. "It seemed like the right thing to do."

We would leave footprints going down the beach, so instead we decided to go into the forest. The idea was mainly to get away from Karen, so it couldn't hurt to be behind a lot of trees.

After that, we ran for a long time, but eventually we had to slow down because neither of us were any good at running marathons.

"How far do you think we should go?" I asked.

"I don't know, but I'm sort of claustrophobic in the trees."

It was so dark, all we could see was foliage, or the blanket it formed against the night. Occasionally, from up above, bits of light climbed down through the leaves, but not often. We ran into branches or trunks like fifty times, which hurt, and it seemed like we would never catch our breath, even if we were still breathing.

We stopped when we'd reached a clearing. For about twenty feet around us, there was nothing, except ground.

"Are you all right?" Michelle said.

"Yeah," I said, "I suppose."

I sat down and looked at her. She moved and I heard her breathing.

"I can't believe this," I said. "It's really… wrong."

"It's kind of weird though. The thing is, I think we've seen Mathew die so many times there isn't really much sympathy left, you know what I mean?"

"Yeah." I nodded.

"What's up with that?"

"I don't know. I really don't."

I listened to make sure there was no one around us. We couldn't light a fire because if we did Karen would find us. I tried to pay attention but it was like I couldn't hear anything at all.

"There has to be something wrong with Karen," Michelle said. "She was never like this before."

"When we get back… if we ever get back, Mathew says he knows what to do about it. I'm just not sure what he means."

"That's very heroic of him."

"Well, in his case, it's more just self-preservation, really." She paused.

"He really hates her, doesn't he? Mathew, I mean."

"Yeah," I said. "I understand why, but it's sad, really." Michelle sighed.

"I haven't been thinking about it much," she said, "but it's all her fault that we're here. She did this just to ruin his trip for him."

"I know. It's strange."

"She's not safe anymore. There's something wrong with her, ever since she took the demon's heart."

We sat for a while and she put her head against my neck.

"Oi!" said a voice, from within the trees. "Oi!"

"Redbeard?" I said. "Is that you?"

"Aye. Tis me."

"How did you get out? I went to give you some food a little while ago and you weren't there."

"I dinnae escape. Tis too complicated a thing to explain in moments."

"Well, I'm glad you're all right."

"I take it ye are with the lass?"

"We aren't going to have to fight you to the death, are we? I'm really not in the mood."

"Nay. I've not got the motivation, nor the energy."

He took a step forward, but I could only make out a floating beard in the darkness.

"Ye must get off this island as soon as possible. Tis not safe here."

"We noticed," I said. The only thing I didn't say is I didn't know whether we should take Karen with us.

I hadn't made up my mind yet, and neither had Michelle.

"There is a boat," he said, "on the other side of the island. Ye must get to it as soon as possible."

"Michelle's asleep," I said. "Do you think I should wake her up?"

"She's coming." Redbeard's voice rasped.

"There's no way. Already?"

"This very moment," he said. "Ye must go, now!"

Karen stabbed a spear through Redbeard's face, except it didn't touch him, because he was just a floating ghost-beard.

I'm not sure what exactly had killed him, but yeah, he'd been telling the truth.

"I could SMELL you," Karen said, "from all the way across the ISLAND!"

Then she threw the spear, so that it passed right through Redbeard's stomach. It sort of nicked my face and stuck into a nearby tree, so that it quivered.

Michelle was awake now.

Somehow, I thought to grab the spear before we ran. If I hadn't, she would have been able to throw it again, and we never would have gotten anywhere at all.

Redbeard had told us to go in a certain direction, but I'm not sure if that was where we went. I heard Karen leaping through the trees above us. The branches rustled and leaves fell down into our faces.

There was no thought to it. We just ran.

Sometimes, she would leap down to chase us along the ground. One time I looked back and she was running on all fours.

Then Karen leapt at me, from just a few feet behind, and because I was holding the spear, the end of it impaled her through the stomach.

I could feel her weight on the end of it, and when her face opened up, with shock, I thought about how familiar she looked, and how she was still kind of great, even if she was trying to kill us.

Of everything that happened on the island, this is the moment I remember most clearly: how the moon was on her face, and she looked at me like—*Guys, relax, I'm only trying to eat you,* and, worse, *How can you do this to me, didn't we love each other for a while?*

I still think about that face, sometimes, and with time I've been adding new things. New thoughts, new regrets. I stood there, holding up the weight of her body, until Michelle grabbed my hands and I kept running; but it was a long, scary moment, an endless, frozen time, and those memories are always the strangest, I think.

They're so big, but also so small.

I know we shouldn't have, because Karen was our friend, but Michelle and I kept running. If we left Karen out here, we knew she would die—from blood loss or just from being in a forest—but we didn't have a choice.

After a while, we slowed down to walk again. My entire body felt cold. Our hands shook where we held them.

"Do you think we're going towards the beach?" I asked.

"Maybe."

After for so long, I could hardly stand. Michelle was doing better than I was.

I've really admired her, always, but right then especially.

Finally, the line of the trees broke, and we were back on the beach, beneath stars.

It seemed like we'd been in the forest for a really long time, but the island probably wasn't very big, especially if we'd crossed it so quickly. I felt like it should have been light by now, but it might only have been dark for a few hours.

"Will we be all right sleeping here?" I said.

"I don't know," said Michelle.

Both of us fell down in the sand.

We slept.

The next morning, when we woke up, it was already noon. We sat for a while, and Michelle caught a fish with her hands, which was awesome. We didn't manage to cook it, but we made leaf-sushi that was actually pretty good.

Then we walked along the beach, holding hands, until we saw the boat Redbeard had mentioned up ahead. It was small, barely big enough for two people, and no motor, only paddles. But we had to take what we could get.

Except we didn't get in the boat immediately. For a while we just stood outside it drawing pictures in the sand.

First, Michelle drew a picture of Redbeard.

"He wasn't so bad in the end," I said. "You know, even with the stuff about the eyes."

I drew a picture of Mathew, and both of us were sad, because it was like we weren't looking at the same person, and we knew that the next time we saw him, nothing could be the same. That just happens, when you're killed and eaten by your own sister, but it was still a shame.

I drew a picture of Karen, and once, we even took a step towards the forest.

"She's still there," Michelle said. "We could help her, if we wanted."

But she took a step back, and I nodded.

"Yeah," I said. "We can't."

We stayed outside the boat for a little longer, drawing pictures, but eventually there was no one else to draw, and no one we could take with us.

Waves.

Leaving the island without supplies had not been a very good idea. If Karen had been with us, she might have been able to wrestle a swordfish and eat it or something, but Michelle and I have never been able to do things like that.

We sat together in the center of the boat, so small that was the only room we had, and looked out at the water. I won't say it was beautiful, because that wasn't what I was thinking about, but I'm sure it probably was, just a little.

"So," I said, "how do you feel?"

"I don't know. Dying like this doesn't seem so bad."

"Am I good company?"

"I suppose. You're not bad, at least."

"Do you wish it was Mathew here, instead of me?"

She turned for a second, and shook her head.

"I used to really like Mathew," she said. "I'm not sure about that, now. It's complicated, you know? Feelings and stuff."

I nodded, even though she wasn't looking at me.

No birds flew through the sky.

"Would it be all right," I said, "if I asked what you've

been thinking about the last few days? You've been really out of it."

"I'd really rather not talk about it. It's not worth the trouble."

I turned over so we were facing each other. The bright light made her skin impossibly pale. We were surrounded by white in this furnace of an ocean.

"Are you sure?" she asked. "I don't think you really want to know."

"I want to know."

"Well, the thing is, I feel like there's something I'm not remembering. I've wanted to ask you about it for a while, but I couldn't bring myself to, because it's not something I want to think about."

"What do you mean?"

We were teetering over a cavern. There was no going back now.

Looking down, I had no idea what I saw.

"I don't have any memories," she said, "from before. I mean, like, all I remember is 'us', at school. I've been trying really hard to find something else, but that's all there is."

"Yeah," I said. "I know what you're talking about."

"You do?"

"All we do is just stay in this place—living and thinking for nothing, without going anywhere. That's all that's left of us."

Silence for a second. Our sides were touching, and I had trouble thinking about anything else.

"Is it because we're characters in a book?" she asked. "Is that why things are like this."

"No," I said. "There was something before. I'm just not sure what it is, anymore."

"When stuff like this happens, I'm not sure what to think."

"Yeah," I said. "Me neither."

Hours later, we were still lying on the bottom of the boat. I heard the water beneath us. Otherwise, even if we were still moving, I might have forgotten about it.

"Hey," I said. "Are you still awake?"

"Mhm."

"Do you mind if I tell you something I really shouldn't? That would maybe make things awkward."

"I don't mind."

"Well, you know when I asked what you were thinking about? This is going to sound really bad, but I was hoping it was me."

"No, I understand."

"That must sound really bad, doesn't it?"

"Sort of. I'm not sure, but I think I might still be angry at you, a little."

"It's my fault. I wasn't really sure how to tell you, but I'm sorry."

"Why did you ever think something between Karen and you would work? It was a ridiculous idea, in the first place."

"I didn't. In the beginning I felt sort of sorry for her.

After that, I'm not sure."

"I think I forgive you, maybe. Do you think I should?"

"I don't know. If you did, it would make me glad."

"We've died together before, and we're about to do it again. I guess that qualifies as a decent bonding experience."

"I suppose."

"What do you want me to do?"

"If you let me kiss you," I said, "it would make me happy."

"What if I said no?"

"I would still want to kiss you."

"I'd like that," she said, "except both of our lips are dry. It would feel funny, if we kissed."

"I don't mind," I said. "I wouldn't mind at all."

Teeth, corpses, dandelions—part I

Karen had been gone for a long time, and eventually we got used to life without her. Except Mathew was still burning her pictures and slicing them in half with weapons, and tossing them into places full of decomposing animals, and probably other stuff I don't even want to think about.

"You know," I told him, "that's really not healthy, right?"

Whenever Karen was mentioned, little sparks of fire came into Mathew's eyes, and he turned into a beast.

Mathew went everywhere with a rocket launcher now. Sometimes he spent all day outside shooting grenades at birds and trees and laughing maniacally.

"No," he said. "I suppose it isn't."

To be honest, I still missed Karen a little, but I didn't tell Mathew, since it could probably have a bad effect on our friendship. And honestly, we weren't sure if we wanted her to come back.

I hadn't seen Mathew much recently. He was lost in his own little world, of hatred and pornography.

Instead, I was spending all my time with Michelle— and even if this was infinitely better, it still made things feel off a little, since it was only two people, and two people make a smaller world than four.

One time, when Michelle and I were out walking, we saw Siguard running an ice-cream stand, and I went up and threw a rock so that it hit him in the face. His teeth were already broken, but he brought both hands to his lips and wailed a little. They came away with blood on them.

A lot of people were standing in line, and all of them looked at me funny. No surprise. Siguard spat blood and wiped away a single tear. He was still pasty as fuck—like a lump of dough with dirt on it, left to cool on some salty ocean rock.

"You don't understand!" he said. "I'm reformed. I love children now. I love sweet things."

About then a kid standing nearby spat out a razorblade.

Siguard shifted a little. He lifted both hands in front of his face and took a step back.

"...Everybody makes mistakes," he said.

Siguard was wearing a shirt with a picture of a tree on it. Beneath the tree there was a dead giraffe. It would have been sort of cute really, if the giraffe hadn't been in so much pain.

"I passed a health inspection," he said, "you know. Once."

"Who conducted it? You, I bet."

"Thoroughly!"

I looked over, and Michelle was sort of wrinkling her nose, in a cute way. She'd always hated Siguard, so much she didn't want to talk to him. It had been her idea for me to throw the rock at him. I don't usually throw rocks at people.

"The last time I saw you," I said, "you were still reformed. What happened?"

"Well, one day Mathew blew me up with a rocket, and then I sort of had a relapse. I started abducting kids and eating them. I went back to baking cake all the time."

"You're terrible. It's a shame you ever stopped smoking crack."

Though I could still see the shaking in his hands sometimes, especially when he held them up like that.

"I only do what I love!" Siguard cried; and then, in a strained, sad voice, he whined: "I only do what makes me happy."

I kept making an effort to hang out with Mathew. It was obvious—he wanted me to choose between him and Karen, even now that she was gone, and it was awkward.

"So how have you been?" he asked.

"Good," I said. Since the last time I'd been in his room, a lot had changed. There were weapons hanging everywhere, combat gear, stuff like that.

Mathew wore a tanktop and military pants. He was smoking a massive cigar.

"It looks… really different in here," I said.

"I'm sick of it. Every time something happens, it's always me who gets hurt. I'm not letting that happen again."

"Just, well… you know, don't change so much you forget what really matters."

"It's fine," he said. "I'm feeling good about myself. I'm feeling like an anti-hero."

"That's good, I guess."

He paused to draw heavily on the cigar. It filled his room with its own distinct odor, a heavy cloud I associate with old men and thick mustaches, curling over broad faces with low-hanging jowls—yes, "jowls", like on a bulldog, except not, and at the same time: exactly.

"Oh yeah," I said. "Michelle was saying that if we had the chance, we should all get together, like we used to do before. Would that be cool?"

"It would be nice," he said, "if I have the time."

There was no longer a bed in his room. Mathew slept on a weight bench now.

Everyone is disappearing, I thought. *Everyone is turning into a scary person.*

After class got out, I walked through the halls. My legs hurt and so did my back, from sitting in a desk so long.

I sat down in the cafeteria, where Michelle was supposed to meet me in like an hour. The cafeteria was full of people eating and studying and looking at things on their laptops—no surprise.

I had a book with me that I didn't feel like reading. I should probably have been studying but I never study unless I can possibly help it.

There was a commotion on the other side of the cafeteria, a mess of people shouting and running away. I looked over there to see Siguard again, except now he was crawling on the ground with blood coming out of his mouth.

He went towards one girl and started chewing on her leg. He tore off strips of it and swallowed them down his throat. I'd seen him do almost the same thing before, but it was different, now. Nothing remained in him, except hunger, for happiness or humanity or whatever. But no matter what it was, he wouldn't find it.

If there had been a security guard or someone with a

gun, they might have shot Siguard once, except even after he fell on the ground, he would get back up eventually.

Unless Siguard had been shot in the brain, he would get up again, again and again, no matter what.

I went out towards the entrance, and Mathew was there already, holding two huge machine guns, one in each hand, shooting zombies in the face.

He was wearing an army-patterned tanktop, with a bandanna tied around his forehead. Sweat dripped down towards his eyes, both of them strained with effort.

A mass of zombies flowed into the building from outside, wearing sweaters and polo and tastefully folded scarves. Their heads jerked back and split open when Mathew shot them. When he threw a grenade, the zombies splattered into a soup of severed limbs and burning organs.

More zombies spilled in. There was nothing outside but another horde of zombies.

"Come on," I said. "We have to go!"

Mathew shot until one of his guns was out of ammo. Using it like a spear, he shoved the tip through another zombie's chest, and pulled a shotgun from his back.

He also had twin machetes and a chainsaw.

"Just go on," he said. "I'll hold them off here."

"No way. You'll die."

"That's fine." Others zombies were coming from behind me, even as he tried to clear a path. "It's just... I don't know, I need to do this. Not for you or anyone else, but for myself. Does that make sense?"

"Yeah, I guess."

"Then get the fuck out!" In one move, he knocked four of them down. "There isn't much time!"

I wanted to tell him, then, that I really appreciated what he was doing—that I really appreciated everything he'd done, even if I rarely got a chance to tell him—but even if I had, it wouldn't have done anything, because I didn't have the time.

There was no time for anything anymore, even in a world standing still.

Upstairs, everything seemed a little better, but I wasn't sure where to go. Zombies ran out around corners, holding both arms in front of them and moaning. Every time, I would hit them like ten times in the face with a folding chair, until the skull sloughed off and purple goop spilled out.

At one point, I saw the samurai in a circle of zombies, cutting them in half and doing backflips. For a second, I thought of joining him, but despite being the main character of this book (at least I think I am), I doubted he'd have much interest in saving me, since I would only slow him down.

There was nowhere to go, so I just went inside a classroom and locked the door. It was out of the way, so hopefully they would leave me alone.

I sort of barricaded the door, but it got boring halfway through, so I did a shitty job.

After that, all I could do was sit, staring out the window. All the streets were full of people eating each other, or being eaten.

It wouldn't get dark for hours.

I sat in that room all day, and—to be honest—I was glad to be there. I needed a time-out, a safe space; to just think, or remember, or whatever. So I sat and watched the sun as people got eaten outside, and I thought: it's painful, to think about the past, when it's so different from the present.

I wanted to remember sometime before, when all of us were still friends—when it seemed like everything had a place in the world, and that place was right, it was good, it was where things should be... and nothing could come between us; or at least we thought it couldn't, even if eventually it would.

final dungeon adventure fantasy quest
(a beautiful memory)

This is the story of the time we fought the Lord of Darkness, and it was badass as hell.

The time came when, hearing word of the darkness looming outside The City, the hero of our story—Mathew, a level one warrior—decided he wanted to cut it in half with a sword.

"It'll be fun," he said. "You know, like a video game."

"Hmm," I said. "Well, I do like playing video games."

We were in my apartment. Mathew had come in holding a huge sword over his shoulder, except it was so heavy he could barely carry it.

"Right," he said. "So, first we should go recruit an adventuring party. I've already talked to Karen—she'll meet us outside The City. She's busy practicing."

This was a long time ago, when the things Mathew said about Karen were mostly just stories, even after what I'd seen her do to Siguard.

"There's a store near here where we can buy you a weapon," Mathew said.

"Cool. I don't have any weapons right now."

"And then we should stop by the village elder. He'll tell us important things."

"Yeah. The village elder."

We didn't talk about him much, but of course he was there, because every City has a village elder.

Outside, in the streets, all anyone could talk about was the Lord of Darkness. Along the way, we passed a man pacing back and forth in front of our apartment building. As he spoke, words appeared floating over his head.

"The Dark Lord's armies are in the east!" exclaimed the man. "He's destroyed villages, slain kings. What are we to do? Oh!" The man let out a cry, all in capital letters. "WHAT ARE WE TO DO? We need heroes to save us!"

Mathew gestured to the man with his sword.

"He's been repeating the same thing for hours. And watch—look at this."

That whole time, the man was just walking in place, exactly like a character in an old video game.

"He must have a lot on his mind," I said. "That was very topical."

"Yeah," said Mathew. "It was nice of him. It's like he's telling us what we need to know."

Down the street, everyone we passed kept telling us things. Most of them were talking about the Dark Lord, except a few who wanted to greet us as travelers.

"Everyone is so nice today," Matthew said.

"I don't know. Isn't it a little weird how they keep walking in place?"

"Nah. It's not like they have anything better to do, right?"

At one point, a woman ran up and blocked our path.

"These are for you!" she said, and handed us two health potions. They were little red bottles with the words "health potion" written on the side.

"Thanks!" I said. "This is sure to be very useful."

Mathew nodded and put the health potion in our adventuring pack.

The village elder lived in a small, one-room hut somewhere in The City, with a dirt floor and barely any furniture. He was an old man with a long white beard, wearing purple robes and walking with his back stooped.

"You've come," he said. "Hero."

The village elder walked forward, and took Mathew's hand. Mathew had to set his sword down before he could talk, since it was too heavy to hold in one hand.

"Destiny has brought you to us," said the village elder, all the words floating over his head as he said them. "You will save us from the Dark Lord!"

"Destiny," Mathew said. "Yeah!"

"You will go into the lands to the east, where evil resides, and there you will confront the Dark Lord, who lives in a castle. Within the castle are many minions. They, too, are evil and dark."

"Fuck evil," Mathew said. "Fuck darkness!"

The village elder turned towards me. He had a really pointy nose.

"And I see you've already gathered a companion," he said. "A white mage."

I hadn't noticed, but yeah—there were words floating

over my head. LEVEL 1 WHITE MAGE. Which meant I didn't fight; I used healing magic.

"I don't know," I said. "This is all pretty new to me."

The village elder laughed, and the words "Ha, ha, ha," floated in the air over his head.

"You're afraid," he said, "but destiny has brought you here. You are great heroes." Then he paused, and turned to Mathew. "Well, mostly you. But you are heroes, nonetheless."

I didn't appreciate that very much, but I suppose that's how it goes. No one is ever very interested in supporting characters. It was odd, but also somehow illuminating.

I didn't feel like myself—I felt like Mathew.

After that, we walked to the store. Like everyone knows, The City goes on for miles—it's so huge you could walk a whole lifetime in any direction and still get lost in it—but that whole way, there are only a few kinds of stores. Some sell weapons; others sell armor; and then others sell adventuring supplies.

"We both need armor," Mathew said, so we went to the weapon shop first. The weapon shop was another one-room building with a man standing behind a counter on the far side. That man had a very large mustache, and when we talked to him, the words "buy" and "sell" appeared in the air above his head.

Mathew spent fifty gold pieces on a gigantic suit of armor so big I could hardly see his body beneath it. As a white mage, I bought a blouse and a miniskirt, which also cost fifty gold pieces.

"It looks good on you," Mathew said. "I always knew you had the figure for it."

"Thanks," I said. "I've always wanted to fight monsters while wearing a miniskirt. Though I'm not sure how well it works as armor?"

White mage is a gendered class, obviously.

At the weapon store, we ran into Michelle. She was wearing an old-style breaches and tunic kind of outfit, with boots, and on her back was a bow and arrow. Above her head floated the words "Level 1 Ranger."

"You look good," she said.

"Thanks," I said. "I'm trying out the look."

As a white mage, my weapon was a staff with a dildo strapped to the end. It also cost fifty gold pieces.

Then we went to the edge of The City, because it was time to fight monsters.

We walked down the road—a long, straight, dirt path, with rows of blocky trees to either side. We could see the Dark Lord's castle in the distance: a big, dark, evil thing, with thunderclouds collecting around the top of it.

"At least the weather is nice," Michelle said. Now that she was with us, I was feeling pretty badass.

"Yeah," I said. "I sort of felt like walking, anyway."

"Oh nice," Mathew said, and pointed. "Look, there's a treasure chest off the path!"

He was right. It was a big, archaic looking treasure chest, sitting underneath a tree.

"I wonder what it's doing there?" Michelle said.

We stepped forward, and stood around the treasure chest, not opening it.

"Yeah," I said. "It might belong to someone. That's stealing right?"

"Fuck 'em," Mathew said.

Then he opened the treasure chest, and inside it was another health potion.

"Nice!" he said, and added it into our adventuring pack.

Further along the path, we saw a green slime. It was a blob like a teardrop with big, cartoonish eyes, and when we stepped forward, more words scrolled in the air above the path:

A GREEN SLIME HAS APPEARED!

"Right," Mathew said. "Let's do this."

All of us got into a line on the path, standing side by side. Mathew attacked first: he ran forward, holding his sword over his head. He brought it down into the slime, and more letters appeared.

THE GREEN SLIME HAS LOST 6 HP.

Mathew stepped back into line, and he was sort of grinning a little.

Next, Michelle stepped forward, and shot it once with her bow.

THE GREEN SLIME HAS LOST 5 HP.

Finally, it was my turn, so I ran forward and hit at the slime with my dildo on a stick, but it just bounced off.

THE GREEN SLIME HAS LOST 0 HP.

"Well shit," I said, and stepped back into line.

Next, it must have been the slime's turn, so it slid forward (leaving a trail of green ooze on the ground), and tried to head-butt Mathew, except it missed.

MISS! LEVEL 1 WARRIOR HAS LOST 0 HP.

The slime slunk back to its spot, and maybe it looked kind of sad—but, while it was looking sad, Mathew ran forward and stabbed his sword through its face.

CRITICAL HIT! GREEN SLIME HAS LOST 12 HP.

Then the slime died, and started to melt. Music played in the air—a sort of triumphant jingle—and we pumped our fists and gave each other high-fives and stuff.

GREEN SLIME HAS DROPPED:
23 GOLD PIECES
1 LOW-GRADE TUNIC
1 PIECE OF MEAT

Mathew stepped backward, picked up the piece of meat, and started eating it. It was huge, basically like a whole ham, sitting in the center of the road on a plate, with a bone sticking out of one side.

"Wait," I said. "We're not supposed to eat it yet. You have to wait until you've lost some HP."

"Fuck it," Mathew said, and picked it up and took a bite. "I'm hungry, you know?"

We fought two green slimes, then a red slime—which was like a green slime, but angrier. All that time, none of us had gotten hit. We were feeling pretty awesome, like this could go on forever, without changing.

Then:

A WILD BOAR HAS APPEARED!

As we got in line, the boar spat and scratched at its flank. It was huge: a heavy, snorting, battering ram of meat with two horns, kicking clouds of dirt up from the road.

Like usual, Mathew and Michelle attacked first. Altogether, they did 13 points of damage. Then I smacked it in the face with my dildo-staff.

WILD BOAR HAS TAKEN 1 POINT OF DAMAGE.

But, though we hadn't seen anything like this before, more words appeared.

WILD BOAR IS ENRAGED!

Then it rushed forward, kicking up dust, hooves crashing against the ground, and gored Mathew through the stomach.

CRITICAL HIT! LEVEL 1 WARRIOR HAS TAKEN 20 POINTS OF DAMAGE.

"Fuck!" Mathew said, and keeled over. He dropped his sword, and reached down. Blood soaked his hands; and when he tried to speak, he couldn't, because all that happened was he started to vomit blood.

The boar had run one horn into Mathew's stomach, then jerked up, so the whole bag of it spilled open. Mathew's organs leaked through his fingers: dark blue and red lumps, a mess of pustules and meat.

I looked at the words above Mathew's head.

He only had one HP left.

"Mathew is next," I said, and looked at Michelle. "But he can't move. He's dying!"

We turned to look at the boar. After becoming enraged, its skin shone a bright red, like someone had painted it with a crayon. We were worried it would attack again, but it just stood there, waiting its turn.

It was hard to focus, or think, because the whole time Mathew was screaming in the background, and writhing with his face pressed against the ground.

"I think...." Michelle paused. "You're a white mage—you can heal him!"

"Right," I said. "Yeah, that's it."

I poked Mathew in the face with my dildo on a stick, saying the words I thought were right: and a bright white light shone on him, making a glowy sound.

All at once, Mathew's organs jumped back into his stomach, like apples thrown into a sack, and the sound of his breath got less wet. His lungs were no longer punctured.

LEVEL 1 WARRIOR HAS REGAINED 15 HP.

Mathew stood. He wiped his face, but didn't say much. His skin was pale, and his eyes were red. For a while all of us just stood there, not looking at the boar.

"I don't want to do this anymore," he said.

We decided to attack one more time, before the boar had its turn, but then we would run, because we couldn't risk that happening to anyone else.

"It hurt," Mathew said. "I don't know why. For some reason I thought it wouldn't hurt."

"It did 20 damage," Michelle said, "but none of us have that much HP. If it hits any of us, we'll die."

"There's some way to heal ourselves," I said. "Right? I'm a white mage, I can bring us back to life."

"Maybe," Mathew said. "But you don't know how yet."

So Mathew ran forward and attacked with his sword.

WILD BOAR HAS TAKEN 6 POINTS OF DAMAGE!

Mathew walked back to the line, dejected.

"Okay then," Michelle said. "We have to run."

"But what if we don't get away?" Mathew said.

"I don't know," I said. The wind blew, so that my miniskirt came up around my thighs. It was a little cold, but I was so scared I barely even noticed.

"I guess we have to try," Michelle said.

Then, just when we were about to run, a level 50 Berserker appeared.

It was Karen, wearing an immense suit of armor and holding a huge axe over her shoulders. We could hardly see her face, because her helmet was so big. But we knew it was her because she yelled when she attacked, and the boar fell into two pieces, spewing blood and a flood of organs.

CRITICAL HIT! WILD BOAR HAS TAKEN 400 POINTS OF DAMAGE!

The victory music played, and something strange happened. I felt a new energy or freshness in my arms, and I stood up and I just felt better about myself—so good, it was almost like I'd learned a new spell.

WHITE MAGE HAS REACHED LEVEL 2!

I looked around, and saw Mathew and Michelle had leveled up too.

"It's nice," Michelle said.

"Yeah," Mathew said. "It's as if I've gained exactly three points of strength, one of speed, two points of defense, and seven HP."

"Yeah," I said. "It's sort of like that."

We turned around, and Karen was standing with her sword in the ground, eating a piece of meat on a plate from the boar. That's part of the reason why, in the start of this book, I talked a little about how Karen was a *deus ex machina*, since she was always doing things like that.

"You guys," she said. "It's like you always need my help."

Karen took care of the rest of the monsters on the way. She always killed them in one hit, but the rest of us still leveled up, and it was nice. It was a long day, walking along the road towards the Dark Lord's castle, but the road was straight the whole way.

Every little while, we passed more chests along the side of the road, so after a while we had a bunch of healing potions. Mathew found new armor. A metal slime dropped a new bow for Michelle. At one point a zombie monster even dropped a new mini-skirt for me—but no, I don't want to think about zombies.

"You look good," Karen said, and Mathew told me later she'd been staring at my ass all day. I'm not sure if that was where it started, but in retrospect (even considering everything that's happened since), that day is a good reminder of how much we owe to Karen, since even if she was always beating us up, she was always saving us too.

And she looked cool in her armor.

Those were good times, and—to be honest—it's how I'd like to remember us. Karen and Mathew were still (sort of) getting along. Karen and I talked and I wasn't afraid of her yet.

Since this was a long time ago, when they were still best friends, Mathew and Michelle walked ahead of us, and they talked to each other about their favorite things: how they loved pornography, and pictures of dead goats.

At one point, Karen showed us where she'd killed a dragon.

"It spat fire and stuff," she said, "but I then cut off its head, and it dropped this armor."

That made sense. I looked above her head, and saw she was wearing a "Legendary Dragonscale Plate-male +5," and that seemed like the kind of armor Karen would wear.

Her axe was a "Legendary Axe of Fiery Beheading +6," and that seemed like the kind of axe she would carry.

It was a long day, but it wasn't until much later—when all of us were at level 15—that I realized it was unnaturally long. The sun, an unmoving dot, hung at a still point in the sky, and (maybe more than ever, before or since) the whole world was unchanging.

It was noon and it would stay noon forever, on that road surrounded by those trees, full of various colored slimes. Except, even if the world was static, even if it was infinite and perfect and still, and nothing would change and everything would go on, and we would walk down that road forever, leveling up for no reason:

Even then, I was sort of getting tired.

Eventually, we stopped and made a fire along the road. We pulled four plates of meat out of our adventuring pack and sat around eating it. It was good and stayed warm forever, which was weird but convenient.

"We're almost there," Mathew said, and he was right. In the distance, the castle of the Dark Lord had grown much larger, so that we were nearly standing in the thunderstorm that covered it forever.

"It's kind of loud," Michelle said.

"Yeah," I said. "I mean, I don't see why the storm never takes a break."

"It's an *evil* storm," Mathew said. "Obviously."

"Right."

We finished eating, and I looked at the number floating over my head: level 25 White Mage.

"It's amazing," I said, "what happens when you have someone to do the fighting for you."

Karen, I should have mentioned, was off fighting a minotaur in the distance. We'd been slowing her down, so she wanted some time on her own, without the weaklings.

"Yeah," Mathew said. "Well, I hope it's enough. I don't feel like training anymore."

Michelle was sitting next to Mathew on the far side of the fire. In retrospect, though I haven't thought about it much, I wonder if they liked each other—I always thought they did, that maybe they were in love (or something close), but I never did, and when things changed, we didn't talk about it.

Mathew was angry at me for a lot of things—how I sided with Karen over him, sometimes, and how I left him in a closet to choke on his own vomit and die, and how one day I stole half of his french fries when he was out of the room and didn't apologize for it—but he never mentioned Michelle, though I always thought he would.

Mathew is a strange guy, and even if I've known him so long, sometimes I feel like I don't know him at all. He's silly and mostly a douchebag, but he's my friend, and we've had life or death experiences together, and that has to count for something.

What's worse, is now I don't know whether it's my fault, or whether it's his, and it seems like there's nothing I can do about it: that we'll go on forever, and things will always seem just a little wrong, when once they were right between us.

Once, as friends, all of us spent a day on that road killing slimes, and it was the best day we ever had, in some ways, even if a few times we got the organs gored out of our stomachs. We were together because we wanted to be together, and (for the first time) it was like we had a purpose, or a destination, just for a while.

We slept on the side of the road, in the endless sunlight, and nothing scared me for a while.

We fought our way to the Dark Lord's castle. Karen killed giants. She killed three-headed walruses. She killed a massive, penis shaped cyclops, with gobs of semen leaking from its (one) eye, and a wrinkly, hanging pouch—like a ballsack—for its stomach.

It was dark and stormy outside, but the doors of the castle stood open. It was a massive, gothic spiral of jutting pillars and interlinked bridges—but, after Karen crossed the moat, and killed the hundred soldiers outside, all we had to do was walk inside, into the Dark Lord's audience chamber.

He sat in a throne at the back of a huge room, lined with pillars to every side. Torches burned on the walls, with suits of armor for decoration, and all the kind of things you'd expect to see in a castle.

"Fools!" cried the Dark Lord, and rose from his throne. He wore a dark robe, and his voice was evil. "How dare you enter my FORTRESS OF DARKNESS?"

The Dark Lord paced from side to side.

"You ought to know," he said, "no hero stands a chance against my FIRE-BREATHING DRAGON."

A dragon flew down from the ceiling, breathing fire. We all stood in a line in front of it. I'd never seen a dragon before. Flames leaked from its mouth, and its wings folded elaborately at its back. The dragon's scales were red. Its eyes glowed yellow.

Theatrical music played in the background. Words showed up in the air, and it was kind of epic.

A FIRE-BREATHING DRAGON HAS APPEARED!

The dragon roared. Clouds of fire billowed from its nostrils. It looked at us—me in particular, because of the mini-skirt—its eyes like feral diamonds, and its expression said: White Mage, I will breathe on you, and I will eat you, and no healing potion will protect you from me burning and eating you.

I should mention that I was scared, because I was pretty scared.

Then Karen leapt into the air, and—with her Legendary Axe of Fiery Beheading +6—she cut off the dragon's head.

All the usual stuff happened: our victory music played, and all of us leveled up.

I was now a level 35 White Mage, and I'd learned the spell "Holy Light," which burned enemies, so finally I could do something other than smack them with my dildo-staff.

A little late, but whatever.

As Karen picked up everything the dragon had dropped, the Dark Lord let out a furious shout.

"How?" he said. "That was a FIRE-BREATHING DRAGON."

We walked forward, and the Dark Lord, standing on his dais, threw back his hood.

It was Siguard—which explained why the Dark Lord had a reputation for eating children's livers. He looked the same as always: blond hair and blue eyes and bad dental work, and really unimpressive in those robes.

"You!" he said. "I should have known you would come for me here. But!—"

Siguard stepped forward, holding out his staff, which had a skeleton on the end, instead of a dildo.

"No one has beaten me in the past," he said, "and today will be no different. I am a final boss, I am a DARK LORD."

A drumroll from the background, as the capitalized words appeared over his head.

"I am untouchable!" he cried. "I rule an empire of DARKNESS. You stand no—"

No chance, I think he meant. We stood no chance; but already, Karen had leapt onto the dais and cut him in half.

And then there was no more Dark Lord.

...but no, this isn't how things are anymore. The world isn't simple like that, and we aren't a team, like we used to be, like I wish we were.

The world is difficult, and it doesn't get any simpler when you're a level 35 White Mage.

This is what I thought about, while I was alone in a room while the zombies attacked.

Teeth, corpses, dandelions—part II

I heard a knock at the door, so finally I stood up, and stopped looking out the window at so many scary people. When the zombies came I was scared of everything, and I've been scared of everything since.

Originally, I hadn't planned to let anyone in, but it was Michelle, and if I didn't let her in I would probably die, from killing myself.

"Hey," I said. "Are you all right? I'm glad you found me here."

She held her head down and she hardly looked at me.

"I'm sorry," she said.

"Why? What's going on?"

"I got bit," she said, "on the way here. I didn't know where else to go."

She clasped one arm to her chest, and even when I asked, she wouldn't let me see it.

"I shouldn't have come," she said. "I don't know how much longer I have. In just a second or so, I'll go back outside, so you'll be all right."

"No," I told her, "it's fine."

"What do you mean?"

"I'd rather you stayed in here. Besides, look at the sun. Isn't it nice? It's starting to go down now, a little bit."

"I'll *eat* you," she said. "I don't mean to but I know I will."

"I don't mind," I said. "You know, it's interesting— I've had a lot of time in here. I've been thinking about Mathew, and then I thought about Karen, but mostly I was thinking about you."

"Are you sure?"

"A long time ago," I said, "when we fought the Dark Lord, we were happy. And then I thought about how we were, so I don't want to lock you out, even if you eat me."

I think she was crying a little bit. In my own body, I was crying too.

"I don't understand you," she said.

"That's fine. I don't think I want to be understood."

Michelle sat down next to me, and I gave her a kiss.

When I looked into her eyes, she was crying tears of blood.

"Don't worry," I said, wiping a red streak away. "We've done this before, and we can do it again."

In just a little while, everything will be all right, almost like it was before.

Not exactly, but almost.

The part with the aliens and the children

This is another thing that happened, while Karen was gone, and it's what changed everything.

Michelle and I were in the park when the aliens came, and suddenly there was a huge flying saucer in the sky, so big we could see it from miles in the distance. It made a sound like a purring cat, which is a nice sound for a spaceship to make, but after that it just hovered there, like a big purple plate with a slot machine on top.

"It's pretty," Michelle said, "but I have a bad feeling about this."

I looked around the park, which was full of children laughing and playing and attacking each other with big sticks. Michelle and I had been making chalk drawings on the sidewalk, because that's a fun thing to do, but it's harder to have fun when there's an alien spaceship around.

"Yeah," I said. "This couldn't possibly go well."

We stood up, and watched as huge yellow ropes came out of the side of the ship, like anchors. They landed with a crash. The streets shook, and a few buildings in the distance collapsed.

Then, carrying huge blue sacks that floated in the wind behind them, an army of tentacled things in yellow trench coats ran down the ropes. Their legs were long, taking languid steps, like cartoon thieves scaling the side of a building. Beneath their coats they resembled praying mantises, but with more tentacles.

The children in the park pointed at the aliens, wondering what was in the blue sacks, since the trench coat people were always handing out presents to children.

When the aliens got into the park, they started scooping up children into the blue sacks. Each one was big enough to hold about thirty children. The sack floated in the air behind them, getting bigger the more children were put into it. Inside, the children just floated around, like pieces of jelly in water.

In one tentacle, all the aliens had a big, metal cannon that they held near their shoulders. They didn't use them at first, until someone tried to stop them from scooping up children, and got cut into three pieces with a laser.

The laser made a sound like a fizzing lightbulb, and the dead people gave off a smell like charred bacon.

They didn't kill all of us, just anyone who tried to stop them. But since half of the people there were parents, lots of them were cut in half with lasers.

Michelle and I were too scared to run, so we hid under a picnic table. At one point, an alien in a trench coat— standing about fifteen feet high, the face beneath its hat tilting a little—towered to look down at us, a sack of children floating in the air at its back, and I was so afraid I almost wanted to choke to death on my own vomit.

Once the aliens left, the park was a mess of body parts but no blood, since the skin was charred shut. We stepped over long, thin cuts in the ground where it had been hit by lasers.

"What we need right now," said Michelle, "is a *deus ex machina.*"

But Karen was gone, and neither Michelle or I were very good at cutting people in half. Even the samurai was gone, and I'm not sure he would have helped us to begin with.

"I don't know," I said. "I feel like we should do something, but there's nothing we can do."

I looked at Michelle, her face so close to mine.

"Shouldn't we?" I said. "Aren't we the main characters of this book? Isn't this our story?"

She gave me a kiss, and it was a sad kiss, but it was a nice kiss all the same.

The flying saucer hummed like a murmuring baby in the sky. We should have run away, but instead we just walked down the streets of the city, which all looked pretty much the same.

Not destroyed exactly, but lots of old people cut in half, and no more children. Cars turned over on their side; walls blasted to rubble. Every time an alien passed, turning to look at us with bulging green eyes that stuck out from their faces, we went to the other side of the street.

Then, somewhere ahead of us, someone shot an alien with a rocket launcher—and it was Mathew. The alien exploded, showering cars and street signs with green blood and bits of tentacle like cooked octopus.

We could have talked to him, but instead Michelle and I ducked down behind a car, like action heroes.

Mathew messed around with the remains for a while. He lowered his pants to take a shit on the alien's severed head, which jerked a little when the turd hit it and slid down one side.

We stayed beneath the car until Mathew was gone, still holding his rocket launcher over his shoulder.

"I don't know," Michelle said.

"Yeah," I said. "What happened to him?"

It really bothered both of us that Mathew hadn't paused to wipe.

We followed Mathew down the street. We passed like thirty aliens he'd blown in half with a rocket launcher. The humming of the ship kept getting louder, until we stood beneath it, looking up, and it glowed with a purple light that lit everything on the street below.

Mathew didn't shoot a rocket at the ship, or try to climb the ropes or anything like that. Instead, he went into an immense hole where the yellow ropes had broken through the concrete, and he climbed down.

"Maybe he'll come back up," I said.

"Yeah," Michelle said. "Maybe."

But he never did, and eventually we decided to follow him.

The path beneath the street was dark. It wasn't a sewer, like we thought it would be, just a narrow walkway with a stone ceiling and metal bars to one side. Michelle and I walked in the dark, holding hands.

"Hey," I said, "I just want you to know, that if I had to be walking in the dark with someone while The City was invaded by aliens, I'm glad it's you."

"Aww," she said. There was a silence I hoped was a smile, and she kissed me on the cheek. "That's nice of you."

Mathew must be somewhere up ahead, but we didn't hear any footsteps. With time, the path angled down. We walked for a very long time—for hours, until it was impossible to know how far beneath The City we'd gone.

Finally we saw a point of light ahead, and when we reached it, the tunnel opened into a stone cavern with a spherical ceiling way above us. There was grass, and light shining down, somehow.

The cavern went on as far as I could see in either direction. Running through the center of it was a wall. It had no beginning, and no end. It seemed we could walk along it forever—like the wall ran from one side of The City to the other, and then back again.

"How is there grass down here?" I asked.

From up close, the wall was about thirty feel tall. I'd never seen such dark stone—a long, smooth mirror reflecting *something*, though we couldn't see our reflections in it. We saw something in that dark stone, but not our own faces.

"Look," Michelle said. "Names."

She was right. There were names written on the wall, sometimes the same name many, many times.

I reached out, wanting to touch it, but Michelle stopped me before I could.

"Don't," she said. "I don't think it's a good idea to touch the wall."

"Right," I said. "I don't know what I was thinking."

From up close, the surface didn't resemble stone. It was just darkness.

"I don't like it," I said. "I don't think we're supposed to see this."

We kept walking, until we saw someone up ahead. It was Mathew, kneeling with his hands against the ground. He lifted his head, brought both hands to his mouth, and blew in them.

He stepped forward, and ran one hand along the wall, touching the smooth surface of it. I didn't look at that place he touched, or whose name might have been written there. I didn't want to see.

Mathew turned when we came close, but he didn't look happy to see us.

"You guys shouldn't have followed me," he said. "It's dangerous."

"We were worried," I said.

"You should have talked to us," Michelle said.

"I don't need anyone," Mathew said. "I don't need anyone anymore."

He took a step to one side, kneeling to pick up his rocket launcher.

"When Karen comes back," he said, "I know how to cure her. There's a darkness in her heart, and we have to take it out. Will you help me?"

"I don't know," I said. "I don't know anything about darkness."

"What happened to you?" Michelle said. "You're not the same anymore."

Mathew looked down, and shook his head.

"This is how things are now," he said. "This is how things changed."

Mathew sighed, and turned towards the wall. His eyes were wide and sad, but more than anything: they were tired. I'd never seen Mathew look like that before.

"We should go back to the surface," he said. "There's nothing else for us here."

I looked over at Michelle, and she nodded. I'd thought Mathew wouldn't come with us—that we would leave him here, and find our way back without him. I was glad he decided to go with us, but also sort of uncomfortable.

"Yeah," I said. "Let's go."

And as we walked, I wanted it to feel right along the way. We would talk, just like we used to, and find something funny about what happened. Except we didn't. Mathew was silent. He walked a few steps ahead of us, then a few steps behind, his head down, never meeting our eyes.

That whole time, I couldn't tell whether he was angry with us, or annoyed we'd found him. Michelle had never seen him like this, and neither had I. A weight hung over him, some terrible energy; and no matter how much I wanted to go back, for things to be how they'd always been, he seemed more and more like a scary person.

The closer we got to the surface, the more we heard the sound of the aliens through the concrete. Explosions. Screams. Deep, shaking booms, like tall buildings falling to the ground.

Michelle and I were still holding hands. Mathew walked further and further ahead. But he paused at a ladder that would take us back to the street, one hand out to grasp the bars, and I called out to him.

"Do you have a plan?" I said.

"What do you mean?"

"The aliens," Michelle said. "Do you know what to do about the aliens?"

Mathew blinked. He tilted his head, adjusting his rocket launcher where it hung over his shoulders.

"There was never a plan," he said. "I never meant to do anything about the aliens."

He turned away, and climbed the ladder. Michelle and I stood, looking up, but didn't follow. He wasn't a level 50 hero anymore, or any kind of *deus ex machina*. He just shot the aliens because that was the only thing he knew how to do.

When Michelle and I climbed the ladder, Mathew was already gone. Way down the street, I saw an alien cut someone's grandmother in half with a laser, and it reminded me of the zombies. Both of them were sort of funny, but only in the most serious way.

"You know," Michelle said. "I think I want to eat ice cream."

I nodded. "Yeah, that sounds good. It's been a while."

We walked until we found Siguard's ice cream stand, off the side of the road near a few small, green chairs. It was abandoned, but there was still ice cream in it. I made ice cream cones for both of us, and dipped them in chocolate.

"It's nice," I said. "Isn't it?"

Michelle smiled, and said she'd always liked the taste of chocolate. We ate a little at the table, listening to the explosions in the distance. We walked down the street. Along the way, we passed another park, except there were no children. There were no children anywhere in The City anymore.

As it melted, ice cream dribbled down the side of Michelle's cone, over the tips of her fingers.

"It's nice," she said. "But not nice enough."

We sat down on a bench in one of the empty parks, and looked up. Eventually, the ropes on the side of the ship retracted, and it flew away. It had taken the aliens less than a day to steal all the children in The City.

Evisceration; the silence

A few weeks later, Karen finally came back.

She'd gone on a rampage, eating people. Mathew and I spent almost a day chasing her through the city—just us, because after what had happened on the island, Michelle never wanted to see Karen again. It was hard work, but we knew the corpses would lead us to Karen eventually.

Mathew was still in better shape than I was, even if he'd dropped a little of the muscle from when the zombies attacked. All that way, he always ran ahead of me.

We followed Karen into a mess of old alleyways. Sometimes we saw her silhouette around corners, or heard her growling behind dumpsters. She ran on all fours, like she had in the jungle. There were bloodstains all around her mouth.

Finally, we came to a parking lot, closed in at the end of an alleyway. Karen crouched down and hissed at us. I don't think she was capable of talking anymore.

It's becoming far too common in this story for people to resort to cannibalism.

"We've got you," Mathew said.

He tilted his head, studying her.

The evening hazed red and orange around us. This was not a good time to be thinking about beauty.

Karen snapped her teeth, and flicked her tongue like a reptile.

"I know what to do," Mathew said, "but it isn't going to be easy."

"If you say so," I said.

Mathew stepped forward, holding both arms ready— and Karen struck. She lashed out, claws extended; but, so quick I hardly saw it, Mathew grabbed her arm and threw her over his shoulder. She went down hard. Her skull rocked back onto the pavement.

"Now!" he said. "Pin her to the ground!"

"I can't," I said. "This is too much."

"You have to," Mathew said.

Everything about this felt wrong. Mathew held Karen's torso down with one hand, but even if she was eating people, I still saw the person she'd been, with Mathew's other arm down over her throat. Karen thrashed. She reached up to claw at Mathew's face; flailed out to scrape at the pavement.

"Fuck it," Mathew said. "I'll do it myself."

He put one hand around his back, and pulled out a knife.

"What are you doing?" I yelled. "We're not trying to kill her."

"It's the only way," he said. "We have to take the darkness out."

Mathew held the blade and angled it towards her chest.

"I can't let you do this," I said. "No way."

But I was scared, and I didn't do anything.

Mathew plunged the knife directly down, beneath her

collarbone. Then he started to cut, sawing the skin open until he'd created an opening above her heart.

Thick black liquid spilled out of Karen's chest, writhing where it touched the blade of the knife.

Mathew reached in so far his arm disappeared almost to the wrist. His hand wrenched from side to side, searching for something. Then, all at once, he pulled out a heavy, pulsating mass: a liquid ball, thrashing between his fingers. He tossed it to the side, and it became a wriggling smear across the pavement.

Black blood spilled from Karen's nose and eyes. Trails of black blood leaked from the corners of her mouth.

Mathew paused.

The black lump, just a few feet away, rose and became a man. The man was almost six feet tall and had a body like a hooked scythe.

His face, or maybe his mask, was pointed like the beak of a bird. He didn't have any eyes.

In the center of his narrow chest was a large mouth. Within the mouth was another eye.

"This isn't the one," I said. "This isn't the one she described."

"What...?"

Faster than I could see, the dark figure turned its arm into a blade and swung towards Mathew. He raised one hand, and the scythe cut it off at the wrist. Then the blade swept down again, all the way through his stomach.

Mathew moaned and fell forward.

He pressed his remaining hand to his torso, blood seeping through the fingers.

The dark figure turned to look at me, inscrutable in

what remained of the sunlight.

And then we were alone.

"…Mathew," I said. "Mathew, are you all right?"

He groaned.

Blood pooled on the ground around him, mingling into the black liquid.

"Karen?" I said. "Is she okay?"

Mathew tried to sit up a little, and grimaced. Karen was just a few feet away. He reached out with one arm, and blood spat from his wrist onto her torso.

He beckoned at me with his stump.

"Could you come over here?" he choked. "I can't. I want to check but I can't."

I stepped over and put my hand against her wrist, then her neck, then her throat, searching for her pulse or the feel of her breathing.

Nothing. I felt nothing.

Mathew tried to stand, except he couldn't. It felt like his guts would spill out onto the pavement from the pressure, he said, and he was probably right. So he just laid there, bleeding.

Eventually, he perched himself up on one elbow, reaching forward with the good arm to cup his stomach. His breath was ragged, punctuated with loud gasps.

"You really suck," I said. "You know that, right?"

"I don't want to talk about it."

He grimaced, more forcefully this time.

"You didn't help her, man. You killed her."

"She's done it to me. More times than I can count."

"It feels different, though." I paused, and looked over to the corpse. Karen had always had a beautiful face, but I hardly recognized her now. "It doesn't seem right. It doesn't feel like the other times."

He stared at me, with murky, lidded eyes. I couldn't remember the last time I'd looked so closely at Mathew's face.

"It wasn't about making things right," he said.

"I feel lost," he said. "I feel like nothing is funny anymore."

Mathew's head lolled back, and he let out a long, pained breath. This late in the evening, the light was full and heavy. He held his mutilated arm up, his eyes fixed on the bone inside his wrist, the wriggling meat all around it. Lines of blood stained all the way down to his elbow.

"Fuck," he said. "So many times and it still hurts. It hurts more than anything."

"That's a shame," I said.

Mathew started to say something, but stopped. He gasped, and I saw the fingers clench over his stomach.

"Say what you have to say," I said.

"It's just…" he sighed. "It's hard, you know. To feel empty."

I nodded, but didn't meet his eyes.

"Yesterday," he said, "I went walking in The City, like I was looking for something, but no matter how far I went, I couldn't find it." He laughed, and bit his lip at the pain. "Isn't that the worst feeling? When you're looking for something but you don't even know what it is."

"Yeah," I said. "I know that feeling."

"I thought if Karen was gone I could find it. Something to make me happy, or complete. Isn't that weird?"

"It's not something you lost."

"What, then? What was I looking for?"

I shrugged. And when I didn't say anything, Mathew started to yell—I could tell it hurt. His voice bubbled and his throat rasped.

"Don't be like that," he said. "Talk to me. Don't be like that."

"Some things only exist as long as we imagine them," I said. "It doesn't matter if they were ever really there."

"Is the problem..." he trailed off. "Is the problem that we're fictional characters?"

Another moment passed, and I almost didn't answer him. But it was so obvious I couldn't believe he'd asked.

"No," I said. "We knew that from the very first page."

Then I just watched, and Mathew died for a while.

Mathew's breath hitched, and for a minute he was in too much pain to talk. One eye blinked erratically as he stared out; the other stayed shut. When he finally found his voice again, it was weak, so faint he almost whispered.

"I shouldn't say this," he said. "But sometimes it bothers me."

"What?"

"Sometimes, it's almost like I can see the boundaries of the page." His stump pointed left, on an arm so weak he could hardly lift it. "Over there." Then he pointed to the right. "And over there too."

"Yeah," I said. "I know what you're talking about."

"It doesn't bother me all the time, but sometimes it does. Sometimes I hate it."

"There are a lot of things I don't like," I said.

"But what do we do?" Mathew asked. "Doesn't it make you feel something?"

So much blood had soaked through Mathew's shirt, the fabric bursting and heavy. His face was gaunt, pale; the lips thin, the eyes glossy. It was the same face, but somehow alien and faded, like it had never belonged to a person.

I couldn't stay here much longer—and honestly, I realized, I didn't want to. Soon, I would walk away. I would leave Mathew to bleed out, and maybe we would see each other again and maybe we wouldn't, but either way, nothing would be the same again.

"It's just what you'd expect," I said. "I feel terrified."

About the Author

Kyle Muntz is the author of *Green Lights* (Civil Coping Mechanisms, 2014). He is also the writer and developer of *The Pale City*, a forthcoming roleplaying game for PC.

www.ingramcontent.com/pod-product-compliance
Lightning Source LLC
Chambersburg PA
CBHW022001010726
47494CB00003B/843

9781621052067